Published by:
Hollygrove Publishing, Inc.
4100 West Eldorado Parkway
Suite 100-182
McKinney, Texas 75070
(972) 837-6191
http://www.hollygrovepublishing.com

10 - Digit ISBN: 0-9840904-3-6
13 – Digit ISBN: 978-0-9840904-3-3

Printed in the United States of America

Publisher's Note
This is a work of fiction. All events in this story are solely the product of the Author's imagination. Any similarities between any characters and situations in this book to any individuals, living or dead, or actual places and situations are purely coincidental.

Book Club Endorsements

"Let me be the first to say that I love Brian Smith's books. He does not let you down. The story lines are juicy and have an element of surprise. If you have not picked up one of his books, do so ASAP - you will be very satisfied." **Tamika Shamberger, President, Girlfriends Book Club, Sacramento, CA**

"Brian W Smith novels are about real people and real issues. They make you ask yourself, what would I do if that was me? His novels hold you from the first page and give you a big surprise (or twist) at the end you don't see coming." **Lawana Johnson, Founder, Black Pearl Keepin' It R.E.A.L. Book Club, Dallas, TX**

"Brian Smith is definitely one of the most creative, down to earth, and humble brothers that I know taking the literary world by storm today. His uncanny ability to bring his characters to life will have you eagerly anticipating what's to come as you turn the page. His characters are so realistic and relatable, with dialogue that is so on point, readers can easily see themselves or someone they now in the same or similar situations." **Trish Buckner, Founder, Bonded Through Books Book Club, Cleveland, OH**

"Brian W. Smith is a prolific writer, who always engages the reader with an intriguing plot that keeps the pages turning. Never afraid to conquer the taboo subjects, Brian provides literary essence which promotes discussion amongst its readers." **Misty Irby, President, Regal Sisterhood Book Club, McKinney, TX**

"Brian is truly an amazing writer who has hit the world by storm. The Distinct Ladies Book Club is proud of the accomplishments that Brian has made with his writing, presenting us with new authors, and his publishing company." **Tiffany Rainey, President, Distinct Ladies Book Club, Memphis, TN**

"Brian Smith is the next Prince of Drama! He makes fiction seem so real. He always has a great story you can enjoy and relate to. He keeps you wanting for more." **Rose Wright, President, SAVVY Book Club, Jackson, MS**

"Brian W. Smith is a literary genius. His writing is thought provoking and keeps you intrigued and guessing until the last page. There is never a dull moment when reading one of his masterpieces." **Rosalynd Lister, President, S.I.L.K. Book Club, Houston, TX**

"Brian W. Smith is a phenomenal writer. When you pick up a BWS book, you know that you are about to embark upon a literary journey unlike any you've experienced before." **Nickie Rosier, President, Phenomenal Women of Color Book Club, Memphis, TN**

"Many authors write books that entertain, Brian W. Smith novels force the reader to think." **Laverne "Missy" Brown, Co-Founder, Readers Paradise Book Club, Cicero, IL**

"Brian W. Smith is a compelling writer that deals with controversial topics with one or more unexpected twists. His books deal with real life issues/characters that all can relate to." **Caryn Emanuel, President, ASiS Book Club, Lorton, VA**

"Brian W. Smith is one of the most accessible and attentive authors; he is a reader's friend. He is very supportive and down to earth and writes about characters that everyone can relate to." **Makeda Miller, Moderator, Phenomenal Women Book Club, New Orleans, LA**

"Brian W. Smith is a forward thinking, progressive author who actively breaks boundaries in the literary industry. His work is fresh and his topics are always impressive." **Nikkea Smithers, President, Readers With Attitude Book Club, Richmond, VA**

"Brian Smith is a brilliant author who gives readers extraordinary stories with fascinating characters." **Lolita Allen, President, Divas Read 2 Book Club, Dallas, TX**

"Brian Smith is one of the most cutting edge and in your face authors on the scene. He will have you second guessing your own beliefs." **Susan Williams, President, Ebony Pages Book Club, Nashville, TN**

Other Books by Brian W. Smith

Nina's Got A Secret

Mama's Lies – Daddy's Pain

Donna's Dilemma

Donna's Comeback

The S.W.A.P. Game

Final Fling

My Husband's Love Child

This book is dedicated to the loving memory of my mother (who was also my best friend), Ida Mae Smith—a survivor of domestic violence.

BEATER

by

Brian W. Smith

Prologue

"Girl, I'm tired of waiting for you to give me an answer," said Todd in a firm tone as he tried to convince Cynthia, the naïve young girl on the other end of the phone line, to have sex with him. "You know I've been patient. I don't understand why you're trippin'. I told you I'm gonna be gentle—I know you're a virgin…damn!"

Todd first noticed Cynthia during a pep rally as he and a few of his friends stood posing against a wall. Cynthia was sitting amongst a pack of rowdy girls that appeared to be doing everything imaginable to attract as much attention to their group as possible. Cynthia stood out amongst the wild teeny boppers because she was the cutest and more importantly, the calmest.

Todd spent nearly an hour trying to make eye contact with her. When he finally got the opportunity to lock gazes with her, he made the best of it. He hit her with a wink, a kiss, and then a head gesture signaling her to meet him in the hallway. Cynthia, surprised that an upper classmen would even acknowledge her existence, pointed at herself just to make sure his flirtations weren't misdirected.

With the confidence of a world-renowned, male model, Todd flashed his charming smile and nodded. Cynthia blushed so hard that her caramel complexioned cheeks turned as red as a rose. The slender framed girl smiled and stood up like an actress whose name had just been announced as the winner of a coveted Oscar award.

As her girlfriends looked on in surprise—a few were clearly jealous—she carefully slid past her cohorts and made her way towards the hallway. Todd, feeling like a true playa, gave his friend dap and then proceeded to the meeting place.

After successfully getting Cynthia's phone number, Todd met up with his friends and did what all teenage boys do—he embellished the details of his discussion with her. The moment one of his buddies questioned his soliloquy, Todd did another thing that all teenage boys do when their mack skills are questioned—he started bragging about how quickly he could get inside of Cynthia's panties.

Standing in front of his crew, Todd boldly predicted he'd conquer Cynthia within one month. Once the one month deadline passed and his penis was still as dry as the Sahara Desert, Todd pulled another typical teenage boy move in an effort to avoid being teased; he lied and told his friends he'd actually had sex with Cynthia. The truth of the matter, three months had passed since he and Cynthia first met and he was still striking out.

If you really love me Todd, you wouldn't pressure me.

"I ain't been pressurin' you. We've been kickin' it for three months, and I've only asked you for the ass two or three times. If you love me like you say you do, you'd be tryin' to give me what I need."

How do I know you won't tell your friends?

"Girl, I ain't gonna tell dem niggas nothin'!" Todd barked. He could sense that his badgering was starting to wear the gullible little girl down. Since his initial request, she'd gone from an emphatic *no,* to *I'll think about it,* to *if I do this are you gonna tell your friends?*

Todd was in full *playa* mode as he lay stretched across the living room sofa with his hand buried in his pants. He massaged his throbbing pubescent penis as if he was the only person in the house; totally oblivious to his surroundings.

Standing a few feet away in the kitchen eavesdropping on his phone call was his 18 year old sister, Kim. Todd didn't care; he had a case of the blue balls like never before. He knew this was his best chance to close the deal with Cynthia, and he wasn't about to lose sight of his objective. The boy was as focused as a hooker at a condom convention.

With each stutter and pause offered by the young girl, Todd could feel his virgin status getting closer and closer to coming to an end. His goal was to lose his virginity before his 17th birthday. Only three weeks remained before he reached his self-imposed deadline; therefore, he pulled out every trick in his raging hormone-filled trick bag.

I'ma let you know tomorrow.

"Tomorrow?" he asked indignantly. "Why can't you let me know right now?"

You see Todd—there you go again. Why can't you wait 'til tomorrow? When you act like this you make me think that sex is all you want from me.

Forgive her Lord, for the girl—and so many others who have fallen for the okie-doke—had no idea how immature she really was. Ray Charles and Stevie Wonder could have seen that the only thing Todd wanted from this child was sex.

"You promise?" asked Todd in a tone that suddenly bordered on begging. "Are you really gonna let me know what you're gonna do when we talk tomorrow?"

Yes. Do you really love me Todd?

"Of course," Todd said as he celebrated silently. He had no problem lying to her. He was so horny and desperate, he would have agreed to stand on the corner and sell tampons while wearing a pair of spandex pants, a football helmet, and a cape if he thought it would get him his first piece of coochie. "Hell yeah, I love you!"

Well tell me.

"I just did."

Say it like you mean it Todd. I'm not just gonna lose my virginity to some boy who doesn't really love me.

Todd repositioned himself on the sofa and started to pour the bullshit on thick. "Baby girl, I can't even lie. This shit I feel for you is on a whole different level… for real. I love you like a ma'fucka."

"If she falls for that tired-ass line she needs to get played," said Kim in a tone that was loud enough for only her brother to hear.

Todd looked at his sister and placed his finger up to his mouth signaling for her to be quiet. Fearful that his potential victim may have heard Kim's snide remark, he laid the bullshit on even thicker.

"Girl, I'ma tell you the truth, but you'd better not tell your friends this."

I'm not gonna tell them what we discuss.

Todd glanced at Kim again and winked his eye as he tried to contain his laughter. Kim rolled her eyes and shook her head.

"Girl I had to go and talk to my mama about you. I told her I didn't understand how I was feelin'."

Todd are you serious? What did she say?

"I'm almost ashamed to admit it, but she told me that this feelin' I've been having is love. Cynthia, this ain't no bullshit! My mama don't be lying. She used to be counselin' teens about this type of stuff."

For real? My mother was a teen counselor. Where did your mother counsel teens at? Was she a teen counselor at the YMCA?

"Uhhh yeah," Todd replied as his lie was starting to get him off track. "Yeah, she used to be a counselor at the YMCA. She used to also counsel for the PTA, and she even did counseling at the SPCA."

What? Why would she counsel at the SPCA?

"Uhhh," Todd uttered as he dug into his trick bag again. "She used to counsel teenagers who were gettin' rid of their dogs and stuff. You know that shit be emotional for some people."

Cynthia was quiet.

Todd started cringing as he bit his bottom lip. Her silence could only mean one thing—she was no longer buying his bullshit.

I've never heard of counselors at the SPCA, but I could see how they would be needed. I cried when we had to get rid of our dog PeeWee.

Todd let out a sigh of relief as he listened to Cynthia's gullible response flow through the phone line. It was music to his ears. Now all he needed to do was get her back on track before she started a thirty minute conversation about pets.

"Yeah, like I was sayin'—my mama is on her shit when it comes to relationships. That's how I know I'm in love with you. My mama told me."

"Oh Lawd," Kim blurted out as she shook her head harder. "If I ever meet that chick I'm gonna slap the hell out of her for being so stupid!"

I love you too Todd. I'ma do it – I promise. I'ma call you tomorrow and we can talk about when we're gonna get together.

"Okay, Boo. I'ma be waitin' on that call," Todd replied as he pumped his fist in the air like a boxer who'd just won a championship bout. "Tell me what I wanna hear."

I love you, Todd.

"Say it again."

I love you, Todd.

"I love you too, Boo," he replied in the most sensual voice he could muster up. "I'ma holla at you tomorrow."

Todd quickly hung up the phone before the girl could change her mind. He was also anxious to end the conversation so that he could run into the bathroom and take one of his *extended* lather filled-showers; the kind that is a hallmark of all boys between the ages of 15 and 19 years old.

With the agility rivaled by only an Olympic gymnast, he leaped off the sofa effortlessly.

"I don't know why you're all happy," said Kim.

"Mind your business! You're a child—stay in a child's place."

"What!" Kim shouted. "Fool, I'm older than you. You think she's gonna give you some cat, but you're gonna still be a virgin this time next month."

Kim and Todd's relationship was not unlike a lot of siblings. They often bantered back and forth, seizing every chance to take a cheap shot or get a laugh at the other person's expense. They shared the same mother, Linda Dean Carter, but had different fathers. This half sibling factor always seemed to be the source of tension in their relationship because Todd always bragged about his father, Kennedy. Kennedy lived in their household and Kim's dad had been missing in action since she was three years old.

The fact that Kennedy lived with them may have given Todd the upper hand in that area, but it's not like Kennedy was worth bragging on. It was a known fact throughout their extended family that Kennedy had fathered at least four other kids during his ten year marriage to Linda. When Kennedy wasn't spending time in the household with Todd and his family during the weekend, they all knew where he was—including Linda. Kennedy could be found across town with one of his baby mama's as he tried to play daddy to one of the four kids he had out of wedlock. Four little boys called him daddy; all of them younger than Todd.

Kennedy's presence wasn't missed much when he did stay away for two and three days at a time. When he did decide to grace them with his menacing presence, the mood in their house was usually uncomfortable and bleak. Everyone ate in separate rooms and no one communicated. Todd and Kim even avoided talking on the telephone out of fear that he would interrupt their call by picking up another line and embarrassing them while they were talking to classmates.

Too many mouths to feed and not having enough cash to do it made Kennedy an unhappy man. He knew that this wound to his wallet and pride was self inflicted, but that fact didn't make the circumstances less stressful and palatable. Although he brought home the bulk of his paycheck to Linda and the kids, he also brought home all of his built up anger and hostility.

Wicker furniture and floor fans were permanent fixtures throughout the house. The broken blinds on the windows did an admirable job of hiding the huge inoperative console television with the black and white television mounted on top. What few luxury items they possessed were refurbished garage sale selections.

As with all simmering brews, an occasional explosion was inevitable. Kennedy's explosions usually came weekly. Sometimes they would come in the form of yelling at the kids. Sometimes it would come in the form of yelling at the neighbors. But, his main method of releasing his frustration was via Linda's face; he used it as the canvas to express his displeasure with his own life.

The weekly beat downs Kennedy inflicted on Linda didn't endear him to his stepdaughter; in fact, Kim hated him with a passion. There were times when she actually contemplated killing him in his sleep. *I wish he would die,* was her only thought when he walked through the front door. On more than one occasion she stood next to him holding a steak knife as he lay in bed snoring.

Not surprising to anyone, Todd had a different opinion of his father. His opinion was rooted in a genetic bond that was unbreakable—even in the midst of domestic violence.

The two of them would sit in Kim's room and listen to Kennedy's rants through the paper thin walls, and flinch as the haunting sounds of smacks upside their mother's head penetrated their eardrums. Todd would usually find himself trying to console Kim as tears of fear and anger streamed down her face.

I hate your daddy. I wish he would drop dead and die. Kim would think and sometimes mumble on cue.

As much as Todd wanted to acknowledge his sister's pain, he often found himself trying to defend his out of control father.

"At least my daddy didn't run away like your daddy did. Your daddy doesn't even give mama any child support money to take care of you. My daddy has done more for you than your own daddy."

The conflicting sentiments caused these siblings to have somewhat of a love/hate relationship.

"Todd, I know you're probably about to go in that bathroom and play with yourself," said Kim. "But, you'd better not forget to come and do these dishes before Mama and your daddy get back from the movies."

"I'll give you two dollars if you do the dishes for me."

"Nope. Tonight is your night to do the dishes. You need to start bustin' those suds because it's almost ten o'clock. They're gonna return soon so you'd better start doing the dishes right now."

"What movie did they go to see?" asked Todd as he tried to gauge how much time he had left before his parents returned.

"They went to see *Malcolm X*," Kim replied as she plopped down on the sofa her brother had just vacated. She turned on the television and got ready to watch a rerun of *Sanford and Son*.

"Man, I got time," Todd reasoned. "I heard that's a long movie."

"It is a long movie dummy. But, they went to the six o'clock show. It's damn near ten o'clock now; they're gonna be home before you know it."

Todd looked at the clock as he thought about his sister's remarks. His father promised he'd punish him if he failed to wash the dishes again. He'd already failed the task twice that month and a third failure would all but guarantee he'd be grounded for the weekend. Todd was not about to lose the chance to join the ranks of the *laid*, over a few dishes. He immediately marched into the kitchen and went to work.

While Todd washed off the grease soaked skillet sitting in the sink, and prepared to put it and other dishes inside the dishwasher, his parents came through the door. They were both laughing and discussing the movie.

"How was the movie, Mama?" asked Kim.

"It was real good baby. Long, but real good," Linda replied.

Kennedy walked past Kim without acknowledging her. She wasn't offended by his slight, the feeling was mutual. He glanced at Todd and gave him a head nod. Todd nodded back—thankful that he listened to his sister's suggestion.

Kennedy and Linda went straight into the bedroom and closed the door behind them. Kim looked back at Todd and rolled her eyes.

"What's wrong with you?" asked Todd.

"I swear I hate your daddy. I really do wish he'd die."

"Girl, you need to chill out."

"I don't need to do anything. He needs to leave."

"Shut up!" Todd replied defensively.

"You shut up!"

The siblings banter was interrupted by their mother's feeble sounding voice.

"Todd, come here," Linda requested from the bedroom.

After wiping a small puddle of water on the counter top, Todd abandoned the dishes and put his flippant retort to Kim on hold as he went to see what his mother wanted. As he walked out of the kitchen he heard a thump. It was the stomach churning, vomit inducing, goose pimple harvesting thump that kids living with domestic violence become far too familiar with.

Todd paused for a second. He was frozen with fear. He looked at the door and then at his sister.

Kim heard the thump too. She leaped off of the sofa with the same amount of agility Todd had displayed earlier.

"Go and see what's going on Todd," Kim urged.

Todd heard his sister's demand, but he didn't move. His fear rendered him immobile; that is until he heard his mother call out again in a muffled tone.

"Todd! Baby, please come here."

"Go see about Mama, you little punk," Kim yelled and then pushed Todd forward.

Todd gathered up the courage to go check on his mother. He walked gingerly towards the door. The bedroom door was only a few feet away from the kitchen, but the intensity of the moment made the hall seem as long as the hallways at the high school he attended.

He finally arrived at the bedroom door and pushed it open just as his mother was calling his name for a third time. When he opened the door his worst fears came to life.

Kennedy was a tall slender man, but he was very strong. He used his strength to pick Linda's puny 110 lb. frame up by her neck. The thump that Todd and Kim heard came from Linda's back slamming against the closet door.

"What the fuck you mean, I can't have none?" Kennedy questioned as his huge hand wrapped around Linda's scrawny neck.

"Let her go!" Todd shouted.

"Boy, you'd better get the hell outta here and close that damn door!" Kennedy barked as he turned and glared at his son.

Kennedy turned his back to Todd. He assumed that his order would be followed without any questions, but he was wrong. The sight of his mother being suspended in midair moved Todd to action.

Not knowing what to do, Todd did what his instincts told him to do; he jumped on Kennedy's back. Todd was tall for his age; therefore, his limbs were quite long. He wrapped his arms around Kennedy's neck—sort of like the *sleeper* move that wrestlers on television do.

Kennedy had no choice but to address his new adversary. He released the grip he had on Linda's neck and allowed her to fall to the floor. His attention and anger was now directed at his eldest son. Trying to counter Todd's surprise attack was difficult at first, but eventually Kennedy was able to reach around and grab Todd's shirt. He even bit Todd's forearm in an effort to make him release his grip. Veins protruded from Todd's neck as he screamed from the immense pain. Kennedy bit him so hard that he drew blood from the brave teens forearm.

When Todd's grip loosened, Kennedy flung him off of his back like the boy was a flimsy rag doll. The scene looked like a low budget wrestling show. Todd fell on the bed, but he didn't stay there for long. As trickles of blood begin to seep from his arm, Todd struggled to stand up. The tables had suddenly turned;
Kennedy was now stalking him like a lion preparing to pounce on his prey.

Linda was slouched against the closet door with her hands on her own throat as she gasped for air.

Without taking his eyes off his father, Todd backed out of the bedroom and into the living room area.

"Go call the neighbors!" Todd shouted at Kim.

Kim didn't move. She was so afraid of what Kennedy might do if she attempted to leave that she just stood as stiff as a statue.

"Don't just stand there. Kim. Run across the street and get some help!"

Todd never took his eyes off of his father. When his back hit a nearby wall in the hallway he panicked. Kennedy lunged towards him, but that agility Todd possessed enabled him to evade Kennedy's grasp.

As fear surged through his body, Todd figured his only option was to grab a weapon to fight off the lunatic he called *dad*. He ran into the kitchen and grabbed a meat cleaver. With the huge knife in hand, he ran back into the living room and confronted Kennedy.

The sight of the shiny blade in Todd's hand sent Kennedy into an even greater rage. The lanky teenager was bluffing and Kennedy knew it. He charged towards his son, and grabbed the frightened boy by the collar. Two quick jabs to Todd's forehead rendered him virtually unconscious. The knife fell to the floor along with Todd.

Kennedy picked up the knife and looked at Kim. She looked as if she'd seen a ghost as she stood there motionless. With the huge knife in his left hand, Kennedy walked over and stood over Todd.

"So you were gonna stab me? You wanna kill me? After all the shit I've done to take care of you. Don't you know that I've robbed and killed to take care of you and *her* little sorry ass?" Kennedy shouted as he glanced over at Kim.

While he stood hovering over the dazed sixteen year old, Linda emerged from the bedroom. Her maternal instincts kicked in when she saw Kennedy standing next to her child holding the
weapon. The fear that usually rendered her helpless was suddenly gone.

"Get away from my child!" Linda yelled as she ran towards Kennedy.

Kennedy turned when he heard Linda. As she came towards him he thrust the stainless steel blade into her stomach. Linda's body collapsed around his knife wielding fist. Time seemed to stand still as he repeatedly removed and then reinserted it into her chest and stomach.

Linda fell to the floor next to Todd. Kennedy's attack continued. It was brutal. Vicious. Unrelenting. It didn't stop until the blade broke in her body. Blood was everywhere. The chaos of the moment was replaced with temporary silence.

Silence prevailed until Kim finally screamed out. She eventually ran out the front door and across the street to the house owned by a police officer. Todd was curled up in the fetal position clutching his head as a lump the size of Mount

Rushmore formed over his right eye. Linda was sprawled on the floor drowning in her own blood.

Kennedy stood there for a moment and then finally dropped the handle. With movement that resembled a zombie, he walked out of the living room and into his bedroom. Todd finally regained consciousness long enough to reach over and touch his mother's blood stained chest. Once he got his eyes to focus, he stared at the pool of blood that surrounded them.

Moments later, the front door flew open as the off-duty police officer came inside with his 9 millimeter handgun locked and loaded. The scene was so gory it even caused him to pause and take a deep breath.

"Where is he?"

Todd didn't speak, he just pointed towards his parent's bedroom. He never once took his eyes off of his dying mother. Kim came over and fell to her knees and struggled to lift her mother up.

The police officer placed his back against the wall, gripped his hand gun, and held it out in front of him as he crept towards the bedroom. A few seconds later he stopped dead in his tracks. His
movement was halted when he heard a thunderous blast. It was the unmistakable sound of a gunshot.

The sound from Kennedy's 45 caliber handgun sounded like an explosion. The officer immediately put the safety on his gun and leaned against the wall. Whatever was left of Kennedy's head in that bedroom would need to be dealt with by medical personnel.

The ambulance and police sirens were getting closer and closer. With her daughter beside her crying profusely and her son next to her in shock, Linda managed to reach out and grab Todd's hand. As the last little bit of life attempted to leave her body she managed to speak.

"Todd, do you see what happened?"

"Yes, Mama," Todd replied as his emotions seized his vocal chords and made it hard for him to respond.

"Baby you have to promise me... Promise me you will never ever raise your hand to strike a woman," Linda insisted as she strained to talk while coughing up dark, burgundy-colored blood.

"Okay," Todd replied as he touched the crimson fluid flowing from his mother to see if it was real.

"Promise me, Baby. Promise me you will never hit a woman."

Kim just stood there crying and trembling as she waited for her brother's response. She kneeled beside her mother and grabbed her stained hands.

Todd looked at Kim. His heavy breathing caused his chest to protrude and collapse dramatically. He gripped Kim's hand and then flung it to the side. "Don't touch my mama!" he snapped.

"What?" Kim asked, clearly confused by her brothers action.

"You should have helped me. Don't try to hold her hand now."

Todd redirected his attention to his mother. "I promise you, Mama. I promise I won't do this to anyone."

As Todd's last words left his mouth, Linda took one last deep breath, and then expired. Todd's words and his mother's spirit met, swirled, and then merged. Todd and Linda's exchange served as a final vow between a mother and her only son. It was equivalent to the type of oath mobsters make when they promise to never snitch. It was akin to a pinkie swear made by two little girls when they declare their friendship will last forever—or at least until they both fall head over heels for the same little boy.

That gruesome night would forever change Todd and Kim's relationship, beliefs, and their lives.

1

Kim

Todd and I left New Orleans and moved to the small town of Dothan, Alabama after our mother's murder. The responsibility of looking after the two of us fell in the lap of my mother's only sister, Aunt Dawn.

Anyone who has ever visited Dothan knows that it is the polar opposite from the rugged streets of New Orleans. New Orleans averages nearly 175 murders a year. Dothan didn't have 175 murders during a twenty year span. You would think my brother and I would have embraced the opportunity to live in a less violent community—wrong. We were bored out of our minds.

Despite our desire to hop on the first stagecoach heading west and leave that saloon town, the truth of the matter was, that small town environment was ideal for my brother and me. Dothan was far enough away from the hustle and bustle of New Orleans that we could attempt to completely heal our emotional wounds. In theory, the probability that we'd heal was increased because we were away from the bothersome and unsolicited commentary of nosey family, friends, and neighbors. At least that was the theory.

Aunt Dawn was in her early fifties and suffered from diabetes. She worked in the cafeteria at a nearby elementary school for nearly twenty years. A blind person could see that the stress of cooking for a bunch of snot-nosed, bad ass-kids was starting to take its toll. Her body slouched over when she walked. Her steps were measured and she always moved gingerly, as if her feet hurt with every step. Her hair was littered with patches of gray, and despite her efforts to comb it down, she always looked like she had bed head.

Living in the small two bedroom house with our partially disabled aunt wasn't the most ideal arrangement, but it was all that we had. Aunt Dawn didn't have any children, but she did have three moody cats. Even if you didn't see the felines, there presence by the faint urine induced stench that permeated the house. Cat fur, kitty litter, and scratch towers were all over the place.

I always found it interesting that the fur color of the cat's seemed to match their personalities. The black cat was named Midnight. That was one sneaky-ass cat. He always looked at you like he was plotting some type of diabolical plan. Midnight had this look in his eyes like he was doing something to you behind your back. I always sniffed my drink and the milk in my cereal when Midnight was around. I know it sounds crazy, but I wanted to make sure he hadn't pissed in any liquids I was drinking.

Aunt Dawn had a brown female cat named Sissy that always wanted to sit on your lap. I hated her too. Sissy was a pretentious and arrogant cat. She was like that friend that just popped up at your house without calling and didn't know when to leave. Just because Aunt Dawn let her, she just assumed that everyone wanted her fat ass on their lap.

The last of her three cats was a huge charcoal gray-colored male cat named Smokey. Smokey was the meanest animal I'd ever been around. There were pit bulls in New Orleans that would have paid Smokey's big ass to not walk on their side of the street.

Smokey seemed extremely pissed about our arrival. He would often plop down on the sofa and then hiss and arch his back whenever he saw either of us. Neither of us dared to try to rub that cat's back or hold him. It was like Smokey used mental telepathy to talk to you. One day I was tired and decided to sit down on the only sofa in my aunt's tiny house. I didn't really want to sit on the sofa because she had it covered in that plastic that always sticks to your legs. In the summer my legs were glued to the sofa, and in the winter my ass always slid off of it.

Before I sat down I looked over at Smokey, he was sitting his overweight butt on the arm of the sofa. To this day I swear that cat was talking to me without moving his mouth. I could hear his little cat voice in my mind saying, *I wish you would sit your monkey-ass on this sofa. I'll scratch your damn eyes out.*

There really was no need for those cats to get so territorial because my brother and I viewed my aunt's home as a pit stop. Prior to my mother's murder, I was preparing to move into my own apartment after my senior year in high school. I wanted to get away from that bastard Kennedy as soon as possible. My mother's death put those plans on the fast track.

My brother was planning on leaving home to attend the school for the performing arts in Pennsylvania immediately after high school. Once we moved to the sleepy town of Dothan and he had to work at the local Piggly Wiggly grocery store, he became even more obsessed with the idea of going away to attend school.

Todd and I needed time to heal. The city we resided in wasn't as important as whether or not we got some type of professional counseling. Truth of the matter, not even the best counseling would remove our scars.

Needless to say, my anger towards Kennedy was at an all-time high. I hated him so much that I wanted to bring him back to life just so that I could kill him again. My anger consumed me. My inability to shake the emotion caused a slow erosion of my spirit.

Like the steam that builds inside of a pot covered by a heavy lid, that anger inside of me was building to a crescendo. Eventually those toxic feelings needed to be released on some thing or someone. As far as I was concerned, Todd was the perfect candidate. He was the offspring and virtual twin of my stepfather whom I despised. Who better to punish?

2

Todd

My emotions were all over the place. I agonized over the loss of our mother. She was my best friend; my only confidant. As far as I was concerned, our mom was the only person on the planet who loved me unconditionally. The image of her lying beside me bleeding and struggling to hang on to life haunted me. That scene was forever etched into my memory; an indelible brand like a boy carving his girlfriend's name on a tree or writing his nickname in wet cement on the sidewalk.

As I searched for ways to cope with everything that happened, I found myself feeling more embarrassed by my father's actions than angry. That's not to say I wasn't angry—I was definitely upset. But honestly, the person I was mad at was still living in the same house with me—my sister Kim. As far as I was concerned, Kim's lack of action on that ill-fated night contributed to our mother's death.

With emotions swirling around inside of both of our heads like mini tornadoes, counseling was the only thing that would help us cope. Our first counseling session was with a Psychologist named Dr. Grainger. It was our first and only session, but believe me when I tell you, we got our monie's worth.

Kim and I sat quietly in the high back chairs facing the doctor's desk. Neither of us uttered a word. We didn't have to speak because our body language said it all. Kim's arms were folded and she looked straight ahead—never once did she glance in my direction. I ignored her too. I sat in my seat and listened to my Sony Walkman.

Dr. Grainger immediately picked up on the mood as he entered his office.

"Hello," he said as he reached to shake both of our hands.

We both gave him a flimsy handshake and head nod. Dr. Grainger didn't seem offended by our aloofness. The good doctor's specialty was counseling kids that had experienced traumatic events - his skills would be put to the test by us.

"Kim, I see that you're about to turn nineteen next month," he commented, trying to break the silence in the room.

Kim acknowledged his observation by shaking her head in agreement.

"Todd, I see that you just turned seventeen last week."

I heard him, but pretended that I didn't. I continued to stare at the floor; the music from my headphones was so loud that it could be heard from across the room.

Kim reached over and yanked the headphone out of my right ear. "Don't you hear Dr. Grainger talking to you, Stupid?"

"Girl, don't touch my headphones!"

"You're lucky I don't touch you," Kim replied with a clinched fist.

I remember looking down at my sister's fist. It was as if the image of her preparing to hit me gave me a flashback. Suddenly, those feelings I'd been struggling to keep contained started to spill out all over that office. I unleashed a tirade. My outburst even shocked Dr. Grainger.

"I don't know why you're lookin' like you wanna hit me," I shouted. "When your scary ass should have been ready to fight, you didn't move."

"What?" Kim asked. She had a good idea of what I was implying, but wanted me to clarify before she responded.

I graciously accommodated her request for clarity. "You heard me. Now you wanna fight, but when you shoulda been ready to fight you *nutted* up. Our mama might still be alive if you would have helped me fight him. Hell, you didn't even have to help me fight, all you had to do was go and get help. But noooooo, you couldn't even do that because yo' ass was scared! Now you wanna act all hard and shit! Say it with me, *Kim; Mama is dead because Kim didn't help!*"

Kim's eyes instantly filled with water. Her nostrils flared and her fist clinched tighter. Seconds later she jumped up, landing a left hook, and my chin absorbed the blow. I could literally feel my jaws shake and my teeth rattle. My headphones fell out of my ears and my Walkman fell to the floor. I didn't fall out of the chair, but Kim's punch definitely caused me to reposition myself.

"You bitch," I yelled, as I jumped up and lunged towards her.

Dr. Grainger leaped to his feet and stood between the two of us. "Please, calm down! Stop fighting right now!" he demanded.

Kim grabbed her chair and slid it another six feet away from me. I retrieved my Walkman and sat down. Dr. Grainger took a deep breath and prepared for what he knew was going to be a very long session.

"Kim, why did you hit your brother?" he asked her, his hands shook as he struggled to write notes in his notepad.

"Ask him why he said what he said!" she replied.

"Okay, if that will help us get to the bottom of this—I will. Todd, why did you make the comment that provoked Kim's attack?"

I looked at Dr. Grainger like he'd just tried to squeeze my ass. He just witnessed her provoke me yet he still had the nerve to ask me to explain what happened.

"Because it's the truth," I replied and glared at my sister. "She's always yelling at me and wanting to fight me. I've never done anything to her. When she should have been ready to fight, she did nothing. She froze the night our mother died."

"You mean the night your sorry-ass daddy killed my mama," Kim mumbled as tears rolled down her cheeks.

"Yeah right—whatever!" I replied. "All I know is, if you woulda ran outta the house and got help like I told you to, Mama might still be alive. At least I tried to help her. At least I tried to get him off of her. All I asked you to do was to go get help. You couldn't even do that. I wish you woulda died that night instead of Mama!"

Dr. Grainger's eyes shifted from me to Kim. The most conflict he'd ever had to deal with during his career was trying to understand why one of his teenaged patients constantly had sex with her single mother's boyfriends. Or maybe he had to convince an occasional depressed middle aged man that his life was not over because he'd turned 50 years old. But, Dr. Grainger had never dealt with anything this intense. It was written all over his pale white face.

The perplexed doctor watched silently as Kim put her hands over her face and leaned over while she sobbed profusely. The guilt she'd been harboring from that tragic night was beginning to surface.

As Dr. Grainger walked over to console her she jumped up and shouted in my direction, "Fuck you, Todd! I hate you and your dead daddy!"

Kim ran out of the doctor's office. All she could do was run—it's the usual precursor to hiding. She jumped into her car, a 1980 Ford Pinto that our mother once drove, and rushed to Aunt Dawn's house.

I went for a long walk after I left Dr. Grainger's office. I wouldn't be surprised if he went to the nearest bar and grabbed a stiff drink the moment Kim and I left. That poor man looked like he needed counseling after that one session with us.

Eventually my worn down tennis shoes helped me get to Aunt Dawn's house two hours later. I could smell my aunt's fried chicken as I stepped onto the porch.

"Hey Auntie," I mumbled.

"Hey, Todd," the rotund freckled face woman replied. "Y'all finally made it back from your first counseling session. How was it? I used to baby-sit Dr. Grainger's children years ago. He's a good man. I know he can help y'all. Where is your sister?"

"I thought she was already here."

"Why would she be here? Y'all went together."

"Yeah we went together, but we didn't leave together. Kim got mad at some things I said and left."

"What do you mean she got mad and left?"

"Just what I said, Auntie; she ran outta the doctor's office crying. I assumed she came back here."

Auntie Dawn looked down the narrow hallway towards Kim's bedroom and noticed that the door was open. Kim never left her bedroom door open.

"I've been here for nearly an hour, and I haven't seen any sign of Kim since I've been here."

She walked towards Kim's bedroom and pushed the door open. I watched from the living room. I was content with sitting on the couch. My moment of contentment ended when I saw my aunt stand in the doorway to Kim's bedroom and place her hands over her mouth.

I jumped up and ran towards my aunt. When I got to the entrance of my sister's room I saw that Kim's drawers on her dresser were hanging out and clothes were scattered everywhere. Hangers were on the floor and things like her radio and her black and white television were gone.

My aunt started crying. I spent the next few days trying to console her, all the while I held onto my anger. My aunt would ask me two or three times a day to explain to her what happened at our counseling session. I kept my story short and generic. I knew that my aunt couldn't handle the truth.

My aunt cornered Dr. Grainger in the supermarket one day and attempted to make him tell her what could've upset Kim so much, but due to doctor/patient confidentiality, he refused to tell her the details. Aunt Dawn was crushed.

Kim was now in hiding and didn't bother to contact us to let us know where she was. It would be years before I would see or hear from her again.

Ten Years Later

3

Kim

When I packed my clothes and drove off in my Pinto that warm summer day, I never looked back. I drove straight to the city of Atlanta, and secretly lived in a dorm room with a high school friend of mine named Nikki. Nikki was a freshman at Spellman at the time.

For nearly two months I would get up every morning and leave when Nikki headed to class. I would pound the pavement throughout the streets of Atlanta for five and six hours each week day searching for a job. When I knew Nikki and other girls from the dorm were heading back to their rooms, I would head back and blend right in.

I later found out that Nikki was a double agent. With her trustee calling card close at hand, she would contact Todd twice a month and give him an update on me. She reported on my health, disposition, and future plans.

My ability to masquerade as a college freshman was going smoothly, most of the other girls assumed I was a student. But, as luck would have it, not everyone was fooled by me and Nikki's scheme.

Nikki started dating a football player—a football player who already had a girlfriend. That football player's *other* girlfriend started snooping and discovered that Nikki's mysterious roommate had a car. This sent up a major red flag because freshman weren't allowed to have cars on campus. That's when the snitching started.

Fortunately for me, the same day I got discovered and subsequently evicted, I was hired by an apartment complex to be a Leasing Agent. One of the perks of the job was that I received a discounted one bedroom apartment. I was hired on a Tuesday morning; kicked out of the dorm room Tuesday evening; slept in my car Wednesday and Thursday; and moved into my new apartment on Friday.

I was a bundle of energy. After six years of leasing apartments and dealing with pissed off residents, I grew disenchanted with my life. Being a Leasing Agent didn't provide me the type of excitement I yearned. I probably could have stayed in the industry longer, the discounted apartment was great. The monthly bonuses I received for leasing the apartments was great too. But, I was a natural born leader. I needed to be in charge. Unfortunately, the manager of the property had no intentions of stepping down. I was 24 years old and I'd already hit my glass ceiling.

I needed more and I knew how to get it—I needed the inherent challenges of higher learning. The challenge was compounded by the reality that I didn't have any family to rely on. Failure was not an option.

While working as a leasing agent by day, I enrolled in night classes at the local community college so that I could become familiar with the routine of studying. Within two years I received an Associate Degree. The exhilaration of starting something and finishing it was addictive. After graduation I immediately enrolled in Georgia State University. Two years later, I was walking across the stage in a graduation cap and gown.

With a freshly minted Bachelor Degree in Business Administration in tow, I quit my Leasing Agent position, and took an Administrative Assistant position with Boxxmore International. Boxxmore was an international software firm. The company had recently gone public, and was now one of the largest companies in Atlanta.

I had suddenly gone from getting yelled at by tenants who were behind on their rent and angry that I wouldn't give them an extension, to stomping with the big boys in Corporate America. I had no intention of organizing appointments, fetching coffee, and screening calls for some executive for the rest of my life. No, I was far too ambitious for that. Accepting an assistant position was just my way of getting my foot in the door.

I gave little to no thought about Dothan, my younger brother, or anything that reminded me of New Orleans and my roots. I was now 28 years old and moving forward with my life. I had a new career and with any luck, a boyfriend would be on the horizon.

Despite my success at forgetting my family and friends from New Orleans, the one thing I couldn't erase from my memory was Todd's comments about me in that doctor's office. You would think that the night my mother died would be my most haunting memory, but it really wasn't. I'd effectively blocked that imagery from my mind. The only time I thought about my mother's death was when I remembered Todd's harsh comments.

On the surface this may not make sense, but it made a lot of sense to me. Todd accused me of not helping. He called me a coward. His words caused me to have nightmares. I often envisioned my mother up in heaven looking down at me shaking her head in disgust.

I guess I was affected by his words so much because I did feel bad that I didn't act sooner. There is absolutely no way for any of us to know what would have transpired that night even if I'd run out of the house after hearing the first thump. One could argue that my mother's fate was predestined. Mike Tyson could have been there ready to protect her, and it wouldn't have helped. She was supposed to die—period.

Nevertheless, that didn't stop me from waking up from a sound sleep, in a cold sweat, at least once a week. The reoccurring nightmare went on for a decade. They were vivid. They were consistent. Each one ended with my mother looking at me shaking her head in disappointment. My haunting dreams were real, and as far as I was concerned, they were fueled by Todd's mean-spirited remarks during our session with Dr. Grainger.

4

Todd

After Kim left town I felt bad about our altercation in the doctor's office. In hindsight, I knew that I shouldn't have lashed out in that way. My words were mean; hell, they were downright cruel. But, I could never apologize to her because Kim didn't hang around.

I couldn't sit around forever wondering what might have been had we had a chance to talk so I decided to start charting my own course for success. I lingered around Dothan for a year after my high school graduation and worked at a convenience store. That lasted a month or so before my career there was cut short.

After being chastised for taking a thirty-two minute lunch break instead of my scheduled thirty minute break, I decided it was time to get the heck out of town. I met with a military recruiter and thirty days later I was in the United States Army Basic Training program wearing camouflage.

I spent four long years in the army. When I got out on an Honorable Discharge I took my guaranteed money from the G.I. Bill, and started searching for a college to attend. My search didn't last long because my constant communication with Kim's friend Nikki all but guaranteed that I'd end up in Atlanta—near my sister.

Upon arrival in Atlanta, I immediately started searching for a college to attend. My search started and stopped with one school. After being in town for six months, I was accepted into prestigious, Morehouse College.

I was a history buff and was immediately mesmerized by the all male school's long history of producing African-American movers and shakers. From Dr. Martin L. King to Spike Lee to Samuel L. Jackson, the school's list of graduates read like a who's who in the African-American community. One tour of the school was all I needed to decide that I was going to be a Morehouse Man, or die trying.

Trying to work and manage the academic rigors of Morehouse was a little too intense initially, but I eventually got into a good rhythm. It took me five years to earn my Undergraduate Degree, but in the end, I was able to earn a Bachelor Degree in English with a minor in Journalism. Morehouse exposed me to literary classics like *Invisible Man* by Ralph Ellison and *Native Son* by Richard Wright. The eloquence, precision, and candor displayed by those two great authors inspired me to pursue my dream of becoming an author. Despite my current status, I was determined to one day make writing my full-time gig.

After graduation, I signed a six month lease on a cheap efficiency apartment in Riverdale, Georgia. I worked as a bartender at a local night club five nights a week. I know that doesn't seem like a productive line of work for a

Morehouse graduate, but serving drinks to drunken patrons was actually the perfect pastime for an aspiring author. The pay was good, and it gave me the free time I needed during the day to go to the library and research facts for my novel.

When I wasn't at the library, I could be found sitting quietly in a booth at a nearby coffee shop writing my manuscript. I worked tirelessly on what I hoped would be a classic. It was a story I could personally relate to—a story about a young boy who witnessed his mother's murder.

The names had been changed to protect the innocent, but anyone who knew me personally would know that the story was more non-fiction than fiction. In between daily writing and proof reading, I would pause long enough to take long sips of my coffee.

The scent of the coffee beans worked wonders on my senses. Oftentimes I closed my eyes as I slowly sipped from my cup. During those moments I thought about Kim. *Was she okay? Does she miss me? What would I say if I encountered her in a mall or on the streets of Atlanta?*

Time has a way of healing all wounds. My anger towards her had subsided. I longed for an opportunity to talk to Kim. The desire to argue was gone; all I wanted to do was reconnect to my only sibling—well, the only sibling I actually knew. I wanted to hold her. Catch up on the lost time. Tell her I loved her. Unbeknownst to me, I was closer to Kim than I realized. My long lost sister lived in an apartment complex located less than five minutes from mine.

5

Kim

The Senior Management offices at Boxxmore International were located on the tenth floor. The executives and their assistants were the only people with access control cards that worked on the floor. In order for me to get to my new post I had to be escorted by the security guard.

"Hi, my name is Kim Malone," I said nervously as I stood in front of the security desk. "I'm the new Administrative Assistant for Ms. Rachel Biko."

The security guard smiled and shook my hand. He seemed to instinctively know how nervous I was and did what he could to calm me down.

"Hello, Ms. Malone. I'm Lucas. So you're the young lady replacing Megan, huh? She told me to call her when you arrived. I will in a few minutes. In the meantime, I think you should have a seat and relax for a moment—you look a little nervous."

I was embarrassed by his observation, but I followed his instructions because I knew he was right. Lucas gave me a bottle of water and a napkin. "Here you go. This drink should cool you off. You can wipe the sweat from your brow with this napkin."

Sweat beads had formed along my temple and on the bridge of my nose. It was 90 degrees outside and the clock still hadn't struck nine A.M. My freshly styled hair was starting to droop like a wet flower, and perspiration stains were forming on the armpits of my new suit. It was plain to see that I had the first day jitters.

Armed with only the information I could extract from the company's website, I felt unequipped to handle my encounter with Ms. Biko. I was eager to learn more about Rachel. All I knew was that she had recently been promoted to C.O.O. I didn't get a chance to meet her during the interview process because she was in Germany meeting Board Members. Rachel delegated the task of finding a new Administrative Assistant to Megan—the outgoing assistant. I found it odd that she would delegate the task to her and not Human Resources, but I guess Rachel figured that an H.R. person didn't know what she expected out of an assistant as well as Megan did.

"So Lucas, have you worked here long?" I asked.

"Eight years," Lucas proudly replied as he leaned back in his chair. "I've seen quite a few people come and go around here."

"I'll bet," I replied. I noticed an air of confidence in Lucas' tone. It was obvious he knew the company's secrets. "What can you tell me about my new boss?"

"Come with me. I'll tell you a little bit while we head upstairs to her office."

I sprung to my feet and followed Lucas to the elevators. The lobby was small, but the décor was very impressive.

Huge potted plants stood in each corner. They had to be nearly ten feet tall. I figured they probably cost a fourth of my salary. Stretched across the wall between each plant was the longest leather sofa I'd ever seen. It looked soft enough to go to sleep on and more expensive than my first car. The marble floors were so shiny I could see my own reflection. Even the gold molding around the interior of the elevator was impressive.

"Man, I can see they spend top dollar around here," I said, not bothering to hide how impressed I was.

"Yep, they definitely do it big. Your new boss is probably the flashiest person here. Did you see that big white Jaguar parked in that first slot outside of the building?"

"Yes, that's my dream car. I was admiring it as I walked inside the entrance."

"Well, it belongs to her. Rachel is what the kids these days like to call a stunta."

The slang term came from New Orleans and used to refer to someone as a showoff. These were the people who liked to profile in their fancy cars, clothes, houses. When Lucas said the word stunta I immediately thought of Todd. It was the first time I'd thought of my hometown in months. An image of my brother's face flashed across my mind. My brief reflective moment was interrupted by Lucas' friendly warning.

"I hope you have thick skin," he said.

"Excuse me?" I asked. At first I didn't think he was talking to me, but when I remembered that we were the only people in the elevator I knew I'd heard him correctly.

"Thick skin—I hope you have it," he reiterated. "If not, you won't last long working for Rachel."

"Is she that difficult?"

Lucas chuckled as he replied, "Is she difficult? She put the D in difficult. I've watched her since she arrived from San Francisco seven years ago. She's originally from Jamaica, but lived in San Francisco a year or two before moving here. Trust me, she doesn't have that laid-back California style; she is your typical West Indian workaholic."

"Let me guess, she expects that same type of work ethic from her staff."

"You know it," Lucas quickly replied. "That's why Megan is on her way out the door. Rachel came here as the Director of Procurement. Within seven years she has gone from that Director position to the C.O.O. slot."

"Damn," I replied. I was impressed. "How old is she?"

"I think she's around forty," he replied as he rubbed his chin. "Actually, she will be. I remember Megan saying something about organizing a 40th birthday party for her. Since Megan is leavin', the responsibility of organizing that party will probably fall into your lap."

"Rachel doesn't really look her age. She's a fitness fanatic—she looks like she's in her late twenties or early thirties."

"With the money she probably makes I'm sure she can afford to look young," I replied starry eyed. I figured that if I could impress Rachel quickly, I might be allowed to hang around long enough to glean some knowledge from the progressive C.O.O. She sounded like someone who could be a good mentor for me.

"Yeah, the sista's bad," said Lucas. "I'm sure she earns somewhere in the ballpark of $200,000 a year. But, I wouldn't get too impressed because with each promotion she becomes more and more demanding and bossy."

"Is she a sista?"

"Yeah, you didn't know that?"

"No, I didn't. Well, I figured she was, but I haven't seen or talked to her yet—I didn't want to assume. I've only been dealing with this Megan woman."

"Poor Megan," Lucas said in a sarcastic tone.

"Why is she leaving?"

"She's leaving because her skin wasn't thick enough. There would be days when that poor girl would leave here stressed out and crying. It didn't help that Megan had a poor work ethic. But, the primary reason she's leaving is because she started asking too many questions about Rachel's personal business."

"Damn, it's like that?"

"Yep, it's like that. My advice to you is to be at work on time. As a matter of fact, you should probably come in an hour early in the beginning just so you can get a head start on your daily duties. Are you a Christian?"

"Excuse me?"

"Are you a Christian?" asked Lucas in a tone that suggested I should pay close attention to where this line of questioning was going.

"Ummm, I guess," I reluctantly replied. "I got baptized in the Baptist church when I was a child. But we never attended church that often. So, yeah I'm a Christian. Probably not the best, but I'm a Christian. Why do you ask?"

"I asked because Rachel is a very spiritual woman. She doesn't walk around holding a bible like Esther *from Sanford and Son*, but she doesn't hide her love for the Lord. And she will ask you what your denomination is."

"So, let me get this straight, she's a Christian and still walks around acting mean to people?"

Lucas looked at me and chuckled at her naivety. "Are you surprised?"

"A little," I replied.

"You shouldn't be. Some of the meanest and moodiest people I know are posted up in church two and three times a week."

"This is true," I replied with a smirk.

As the elevator reached the eighth floor, Lucas turned to me and offered one last piece of advice.

"Oh yeah, whatever you do, don't ever ask Rachel about her ex-husband."

"Is she recently divorced?"

"No. I think she was divorced when she arrived to Atlanta, but I believe it was a tense divorce. I believe there was a heated custody battle and stuff. Between you and me, I think Rachel and her ex-husband had a lot of debt and financial issues. That's probably why she moved her daughter all the way to Georgia from California."

"Why do you say that?"

"Because bill collectors have called here a few times looking for her ex-husband. They've sent mail too. They can't find him so now they are coming after her. Megan told me Rachel got pissed at her one day when she caught her looking inside of one of those letters."

"Well, I can't blame Rachel for that. I probably would have fired her too. That's none of Megan's business," I replied with an annoyed look on my face.

"I agree. Just remember that she doesn't have a problem with you opening up most of her mail, but when those letters come here with Lecar Biko's name on it—just give them to her."

"Lecar Biko," I mumbled as I tried to mentally tattoo the name into my memory.

"Yeah, Lecar Biko. I think he's one of those African dudes. I'm talkin' straight from the Motherland. You know the type—the ones that don't particularly care for African-Americans."

"Yeah, I ran across a few of them in college," I said as I recalled one guy from Kenya that drove me crazy in school with his smug attitude. "They look down their noses at African-Americans because they think we are all lazy and ignorant."

"Exactly! I think he has that kind of attitude. So, it's no surprise that when they got divorced he wanted to take their daughter back to Africa with him. Rachel wasn't having that so she relocated as far away from him as possible. But, I don't think moving out here to the eastern part of the country was good enough to escape that dude."

We exited the elevator and walked slowly towards the executive suites.

Lucas knew a lot of Rachel's business—too much. You would have thought he was the person sifting through her mail.

"In all fairness to Rachel, I believe she probably got mad at Megan because she felt like Megan could potentially jeopardize her career. Rachel is the first black executive in the history of this company; she ain't tryin' to lose all that she has worked for because some white chick is curious. We both know that if those other high ranking white folk get wind of her financial issues and her marital drama; they could use that against the sista."

"I can believe that," I chimed in. "Many of us have been fired or demoted for far less."

"For real," Lucas replied in agreement. "The stakes are too high to allow some skeletons to mess things up."

"I agree," I replied.

I remember thinking at the time that although Rachel sounded like she could be a little tough, she was simply doing what she had to do to survive. I instantly admired the determination, smarts, and savvy it took for a black woman to ascend to such a lofty corporate perch in such a short time frame. The last thing I wanted to do was be a contributor to any precipitous fall from grace. Lucas used his all-access badge to open the doors to the executive suites. The halls were covered in a deep burgundy color. The carpets were so plush I felt like I was walking on the clouds. The same type of huge plants that were in the downstairs lobby were also scattered throughout the executive foyer.

The open area had an octagon shape and in each quadrant was a huge office.

Megan appeared from an office in the far corner.

"I told you to call me when she arrived," Megan said as she approached.

"It's no problem," Lucas replied. "I had to come up here to take care of something so I decided to escort her."

Lucas turned to me and shook my hand. He didn't say anything else to me, but his eyes were speaking loud and clear: *Get your ass in here on time everyday; do your job and do it well; and don't ask Rachel anything about her trifling ex-husband.*

Megan looked like she was about to have a nervous breakdown. She was 26 years old, but her style of dress and antsy behavior made her seem 20 years her senior. Her eyes were big and round with dark rings under them. Her hair was oily looking and had a dirty blonde appearance. Her frail frame made her wrinkled clothes look two sizes too big. With chipped fingernails that were screaming for a manicure, Megan's exterior mirrored that of a homeless person.

I examined my predecessor closely. My eyes started at the bottom scanning Megan's run down shoes and proceeded upwards until they reached her tousled hair. After careful analysis, I concluded that working for Rachel wasn't the only thing that had worn Megan down—this girl had to be on drugs.

"Are you nervous?" asked Megan.

"Should I be?" I asked with a concerned look on my face. Megan didn't answer, she just gestured for me to follow closely as she pointed out the key points she'd outlined on a sheet of paper. A few left turns and one long hallway later, we ended up in a huge conference room with a long oval shaped table.

"I only have one day to teach you everything I know, so please forgive me if I'm moving and talking fast."

Megan opened a manila folder and flipped through the pages inside. I noticed that she avoided making eye contact; further proving that she may have been on drugs.

"Okay, there is a lot to go over—so much that I'm not sure where to start. Ummmm, let's see. We could look at the monthly reports. No, that's going to take too long. We could look at Rachel's calendar. No, that can be time consuming too. We could…"

"You know what," I interjected. "We should probably keep things simple. Since we only have one day it would probably be easier if you just took me through the sequence of events you would normally tackle on an average day like today."

I was never long on patience. I'd been in Megan's presence for five minutes, and was already annoyed by her excessive rambling.

I see why she's being released. She is tore up from the floor up. I'm probably gonna spend the first few months fixing shit she did wrong.

"Yeah, you're probably right," Megan replied with a confused look on her face. "Follow me," she requested as she stood up and headed towards the door.

I moved closely behind her as I soaked up every comment like a sponge. By the end of that eight hour day I had a firm grasp on which dates reports were due to Rachel; which folders stored the most important Word documents;

those things Rachel liked done before she arrived to work as well as what needed to be done before I left for the day. I even learned which dry cleaners Rachel preferred her clothes to be sent to.

By the end of the day I was exhausted and had a pounding headache from listening to Megan talk. I'd been there all day, but still hadn't met Rachel.

"So, when am I going to meet my new boss?" I asked Megan.

"You will meet her soon enough. Until then, you should probably focus on everything we went over today. Which reminds me; there are still some things you need to know about her before you two actually meet."

"Things like what?"

"Well, first and foremost, she is very protective of her daughter Danielle. She calls her Cupcake. Let me repeat, *she* refers to her by that name—not you. I made the mistake of calling the child Cupcake once, and Rachel stopped speaking to me for two straight days.

"Secondly, you should never mention her ex-husband's name. She absolutely despises the man."

"What is her ex-husband's name?" I asked, having forgotten that Lucas the nosey security guard had already told me.

"His name is Lecar. He is from Jamaica or Africa or somewhere. All I know is that she hates his guts. Apparently they had a very bad divorce. Rachel got custody of Danielle, and apparently because of her salary, she got stuck with most of the bills that were created when they were together."

"What does he do for a living?"

"I don't know. Based on the amount of bills that come here he doesn't do much of anything. Rachel is extremely sensitive about the subject."

"Should I be concerned about him showing up here one day?"

"No, he has never come here looking for her. I believe she has a restraining order against him. I don't think he can come within 50 feet of her."

"Ouch!" I responded, acknowledging how ugly the situation was.

"Yes—it's that bad," said Megan. "By the way, are you very religious?"

"Not really."

"Well, Rachel is very religious. Whatever you do, try to avoid discussions about religion. She doesn't seem eager to embrace the ideas of people who don't claim to be Christians."

"Just my luck, a Christian with no tolerance for others," I replied.

"Yes—ironic isn't it? The foundation of Christianity is supposed to be love, patience, and tolerance; yet, most Christians denounce anyone who has an opposing view. No matter how good a person you are or how well you treat other people, you aren't as good as them if you believe in Buddha or Allah."

"I agree with you on that point," I replied. That was by far the wisest thing Megan had said all day. "Christians can be the biggest hypocrites on earth. But, if you're telling me I have to downplay my views on religion to keep my job, then that's what I will do."

"Good. I strongly recommend that you keep your religious views to yourself. Now we need to talk about one last thing."

"There's more?"

"Yes, and it's big. Rachel is turning 40 years old in about two weeks. She wants to celebrate with a party and she wants it to be very classy. She insisted on inviting several executives from the company as well as some people that work for our competitors. She even asked me to invite a few of the hourly employees around her so that she wouldn't come across as snooty. I've already booked the location."

"What's the name of the venue?" I asked as I wrote down notes in my pad.

"It's going to be at the Jaguar dealership on Peachtree."

"Excuse me?" I asked, I figured Megan was babbling again.

"She wanted something different so I was able to work out something with the owner of the Jaguar dealership where she bought her car."

"That's different," I replied. I was actually impressed at Megan's creativity.

"Yes, it should be nice. The dealership will be closed for the evening. The guests will be allowed to mingle on the showroom floor amongst the cars and their expensive artwork. This dealership is like none you've ever seen."

My heart rate sped up. This was the type of socializing I'd heard about, but never really experienced while living in Atlanta.

"Sounds like you have everything covered. What will I need to do?"

"You still need to set up the entertainment and get her a nice cake."

"How much is my budget?"

"Rachel told me I couldn't spend more than three thousand dollars," Megan replied.

That's more than enough money to work with. I am going to really make an impression.

"Well Kim, I think I've shown you just about everything there is to know about this job. Now you're just going to have to roll up your sleeves and dive right in," Megan said as she grabbed her tattered purse, her shabby briefcase, a pile of papers, and prepared to leave.

"I appreciate you taking the time to show me the ropes. Good luck to you."

We said our good-bye's and embarked upon our new professional journeys. I left the office that evening pumped and ready to do more work on Rachel's party.

My first order of business would be to meet Rachel face-to-face for the first time that next morning. I wanted to make a good impression immediately. I was determined to present to her a breakdown of where we were in the planning process for her 40th birthday party.

I may have wanted to work non-stop, but my stomach had something else in mind. I stopped at a Subway sandwich shop located a few minutes away from my apartment to grab a something to eat. As I pulled into the parking lot I sat there for a second and let the events of the day soak in.

I'm finally in the environment where I can prosper and eventually blow up. Thank you God!

6

Todd

I love my friends. They are a little crazy and loud, but I trust them with my life. That's no exaggeration. When I was about to get jumped by some fake thugs, my posse showed up and wrecked shop. Their viewpoints on life can be a little ridiculous at times, but I still valued their opinions. Call me crazy, but I wouldn't change them one bit.

"Pass the ball Bub!" I shouted.

"I got this!" Big Bubba replied as he tried to fake out Shakey.

"Shakey you need to give up boy, you can't guard Big Bubba. The Secret Service couldn't guard Big Bubba!" taunted the rotund Bruce Bubba Washington.

Bubba's taunts didn't affect the six foot, one hundred sixty pound, Thomas Shaky Brown as he tried his best to guard the big man.

"I can guard yo big ass, Bub," Shaky replied as Bubba continued to back up against him and force his way closer to the hoop. "All I gotta do is pull a refrigerator out here on this court and yo big ass won't be able to concentrate on nothin' but food."

"Whatever, Lil Man! I'ma about to end this shit right now!" Bubba replied as he threw an elbow and hit Shakey in the middle of his chest.

Shakey must have flown ten feet across the court before he landed with his back up against the fence.

"Game!" Bubba shouted as he made the basket.

"Hell yeah!" I shouted as Bubba and I gave each other high fives.

As Shakey lay sprawled on the side of the court with his back and head pressed up against the chain link fence, Bubba and I laughed heartily.

"Compulsive, you'd better go and help your teammate!" said Bubba as he laughed and pointed at Shakey.

He was talking to Ronnie Compulsive McCalister—the fourth member of my traveling circus.

"Come on, Dog. Get up," Compulsive urged as he extended his hand to Shakey.

"Man, I'ma get his fat ass," said Shakey as he struggled to his feet.

"I know, Dog." Compulsive tried his best to hold in his own laughter. "But you know this is street ball—anything goes. Now, dem fools are already over there laughin' at you. I suggest you wipe your nose, Dog—you got somethin' dripping from it. It looks like Big Bub knocked the snot out of you."

"Fo sho! Can I use your towel?" asked Shakey, still dazed from the blow.

"Hell no!" Compulsive replied huffily. "You'd better use your funky ass shirt!"

As usual, the four of us spent the next thirty minutes cooling off under a nearby tree. That tree was sort of like our boardroom. It was the place where we talked about the game we'd just played; laughed and joked about who made the worse shot; and who'd been embarrassed on the court.

"So, what y'all got going on tonight?" asked Shakey.

"You know where I'ma be," said Bubba.

"Man, I got a ménage set up," said Compulsive.

"Nigga you ain't got no ménage set up!" shouted Bubba.

"Cee, that ménage you say you got set up ain't nothin' but a mirage!" I shouted, causing everyone to laugh.

"So, what are you getting' into Tee?" Bubba asked me.

"I'm supposed to be going to dinner with this little chick I met at the gas station last week." "Dinner on a Tuesday?" Compulsive asked. "She must be ugly."

"She ain't ugly!" I shouted and threw a few blades of grass in Compulsive's direction. "Besides, what does going on a dinner date on a Tuesday night have to do with her looks?"

Compulsive swatted away the grass and replied, "The only women that go to dinner on Tuesday's are women who can't get a date. Good lookin' women like to make your ass wait until the weekend.

"Y'all lookin' at me like I'm crazy, but I'm droppin' some serious knowledge—y'all fools need to be takin' notes. Women try to wait to see how many offers they're going to get during the week. On Thursday's they analyze all of the dinner offers they received, and then they call the dude they like the best so that they can set up the dinner date on the weekend."

"That's stupid," I said. Compulsive always had some dumb-ass theory he was trying to get the rest of us to co-sign on.

"Nah, Dog. I agree with Cee on this one," said Shakey. "Dem ugly chicks will go on a date on a Monday after working a double shift, in the middle of a thunderstorm, while they are trying to get over the flu—they're just happy somebody asked them out."

"That's true," said Compulsive. "You can take an ugly chick to Waffle House on a first date—she ain't gonna complain."

"So *that's* why you keep an ugly chick on your arm Compulsive," said Bubba sarcastically.

"And you know it!" Compulsive replied. "Ugly women don't have any expectations. Just feed'em, fuck'em, tell'em their little ugly-ass kids are cute, and they will pay your rent for the rest of the year. But dem fine bitches; they expect a brotha to wine and dine them on the weekends. Shiiit, I'll tell'em in a second - I'm broke. We gonna go right over here to this IHOP and catch the Tuesday special."

"That's deep," Shakey said and gave Compulsive some dap.

"Shut up, Shakey," I admonished. "You're still dizzy from Bubba knocking your ass into that fence."

"I'm not dizzy. Compulsive got a point," Shakey said, as he mulled over the IHOP theory. "If you want to make sure she is really feelin' you, take her ass to IHOP. If she's really feelin' you she ain't gonna care. But, if she wants your money, she's gonna show her true color."

"Tee, don't listen to these fools," said Big Bubba. "First of all, neither one of dem fools has a woman, so their advice ain't worth shit. Secondly, your ass is as broke as the rest of us. That woman ain't tryin' to get the few nickels you have."

"I don't even want to think about tonight—I'm hungry right now. Let's go get something to eat," I said.

"Let's go get some pizza at that spot up the street," Bubba suggested.

"Bubba, yo big ass don't need to be lookin' at a pizza," Shakey said with a chuckle.

"No shit! We need to roll yo big ass over to Subway. There is one right next door to the pizza joint," I said.

"Whatever!" Bubba said dismissively. "You can take yo ass into Subway and get one of those sissy sandwiches, but I'ma get some pizza. I'll probably get me a veggie pizza."

We all looked at Bubba and simultaneously burst into laughter.

"Yo big ass can't spell veggie so I know damn well you ain't gonna order a veggie pizza!" shouted Shakey who was still smarting from the physical assault he'd received from Bubba.

We left the basketball court in my rundown Ford truck. As the dilapidated vehicle sputtered along, in need of oil, water, tires, and a serious interior cleaning, we laughed and cracked jokes at each other's expense until we pulled into the pizza store's parking lot.

I jumped out and went into the Subway sandwich shop next door to the pizza joint. When I walked through the door I immediately saw a face that I hadn't seen in years—my sister's.

7

Kim

My stomach was growling as I stood in line trying to decide what to order. Subway wasn't the first place on my list to go and get something to eat, but it was definitely the healthiest.

As I stood there with my stomach growling like a hungry pit bull was trapped inside, I heard a familiar voice from behind.

"I don't believe this," he mumbled. "Kim, is that you?"

I turned around and nearly fainted when I saw my younger brother. I hadn't seen Todd in ten years. He'd grown a few inches. His shoulders were broader. His tight fade hairstyle had been discarded for dreadlocks. His voice was deeper, but his smile was still as wide and bright as ever.

"Todd?" I asked inquisitively.

"Kim, it's me—Todd," he replied as he walked up closer and grabbed me.

I stood as still as I did the night our mother was murdered. I wasn't trying to be rude, but I was just shocked. He was the last person on the planet I expected to see.

"Todd what are you doing here?"

"I live here. I've been here for a few years now. I graduated from Morehouse, and now live in an apartment not too far from here."

I was still searching for words. We moved to a nearby table and continued our conversation. Todd was genuinely happy to see me. He couldn't contain his enthusiasm. My response was much more subdued.

"Girl, you look great!" Todd exclaimed as he hugged me again. "Man, I've been hoping to run into you. Do you come in here often?"

"How did you know I was in Atlanta?" I asked.

"I've known you were here for years. Nikki told me you were living here in Atlanta with her in her dorm room back in the day. By the time I was able to get to ATL she had already moved back to New Orleans. That was terrible timing because she wasn't able to bring us together. It feels like I've been wandering aimlessly for years now hoping to one day see my big-head sister in this big-ass city. As luck would have it, I run into you when I wasn't trying."

I let out a fake smile as Todd grabbed me and hugged me for the third time. Awkward couldn't come close to describing the moment. Todd must have sensed I wasn't as excited as he was.

"Are you okay?" he asked. "You don't seem too excited to see me."

"I *am* happy to see you," I replied. I guess he could see the tension on my face. "I had a long day at work and I guess I'm still a little stressed out."

"I'm glad that's all it is because you should be excited to see me; we're all the family we got! How have you been? Where are you living? Where are you working?"

I sat down on one of the many stools that aligned the walls of the sandwich shop. I felt like I was in the Twilight Zone. Todd was actually standing in front of me. To make matters worse, he seemed to desire a relationship with me. I'd been living my life for the previous ten years like an only child. Now my real life sibling was up close and personal.

"Uhhh, I am doing fine. I live in the LeBlanc Apartments up the street," I said.

"I'm familiar with those. I pass them every day. I live in the Village Court Apartments on Johnson Ave, a few blocks down the street. So where are you working?"

"Oh, I work at the Boxxmore Corporation."

"Really? I know some people working over there. What department are you working in?"

"None. I'm actually the Administrative Assistant to one of the Vice President's."

"The Administrative Assistant?"

"Yeah, what's wrong with that?"

"Nothing is wrong with it. I'm just surprised to hear that you are working as anyone's assistant. The Kim I remember always had to be in charge of everything."

Todd let out a chuckle, grinned, and tapped me on the shoulder to show me that he was just joking. I'm sure that the look on my face made it clear to him that I didn't find his comment funny.

"Well, you have to get in where you fit in," I replied in a terse tone. "Look, I have to…"

"Man, what are you doing in here?" asked a huge dark skin man coming through the door. The deep voiced stranger was directing his question at Todd.

"I'm coming," Todd replied. "Hey Big B, come over here. I want you to meet someone."

The mammoth sized man walked over and his eyes became as big as bowling balls when he saw me.

"Big B, this is my sister Kim. Kim this Big Bubba."

"Your sister?" asked Bubba. "So this is the long lost sister you've been talkin' about all these years. I was starting to think you were making it up. How are you doing, Lovely Lady?"

"I'm fine," I replied, and extended my hand to shake his.

"My friends call me Bubba, but my special friends call me Big Bubbly," said Bubba as he shook my hand, caressed it with his thumb and index fingers, and then kissed it.

Bubba stood well over six feet tall and weighed more than three hundred pounds. His hands looked like a baseball catcher's mitt. He was so big and overweight that he probably perspired when he was sleeping.

"Man, move your big sweaty ass away from my sister," said Todd as he shoved Bubba. "She ain't tryin' to get with you!"

Bubba was known for being a comedian. He was also notorious for referring to himself in the third person, and he let it show as he tried his best to mack on me.

"You think she don't want Big Bubba," said Bubba to Todd, as he kept his eyes fixed on me. "Most women think they don't want Big Bubba at first glance, but then they find themselves dreamin' about Big Bubba. Thinkin' about Big Bubba while they're sittin' at a red light. Fantasizin' about Big Bubba early in the mornin' while they're eatin' cereal."

As ridiculous as it seemed, Big Bubba's confidence and overweight swag actually put a smile on my face. I didn't want to laugh, but the dude was hilarious.

Bubba continued with his flirting. "Kim, I hate to say it, but now that Big Bubba dun kissed yo hand, you've been cursed."

"Oh really? What kind of curse?"

Bubba looked over both shoulders as if he was a spy preparing to pass classified documents. He looked at me with the most serious face he could muster up and then moved a few inches closer as he whispered, "You now got the curse of the Big Bubba. Don't fight it. Just roll with it, Sista. Roll with it."

Bubba jerked his head around and looked over his shoulder again. He then looked back at me, puckered his huge lips, and blew me a kiss. I stood there trying not to laugh in his face. Bubba suddenly turned and ran out of the sandwich shop. He looked like a big elephant galloping out of the store.

I openly laughed once he was gone. That was the first time I'd laughed so freely in months—maybe even years.

"He is crazy!" I said to Todd.

"No, he ain't crazy. That boy is a fool!" Todd replied.

"So, that's the kind of people you hang out with these days?"

"Yeah, that's one of my boys. Big Bubba is a bouncer at the night club I work at."

"You work at a nightclub?"

"Yeah, I'm a bartender. I do that at night while I pursue my true calling during the day. I also have a part-time bartending gig at a restaurant too, but I make most of my money at the nightclub."

"You said you have a true calling—what is it?"

"I'm a writer. I'm working on my first novel. Doing the bartender thing gives me the time I need during the day to work on the logistics of getting published."

"So you're writing now? What type of books?"

"Fiction. I may venture off into non-fiction one day, but for now I'm writing fiction."

"You get to use that imagination of yours," I said as I took my index finger and nudged my brother's temple.

"Yeah, I love writing. That's how I ended up here in Atlanta. I attended Morehouse and studied Journalism."

"Morehouse! Impressive."

"Yeah, your little brother is a Morehouse Man."

"What about you? You ain't just stumble into a job at Boxxmore. You must have gone to school or somethin'."

"Yes, I did." I looked over Todd's shoulder. I could see Bubba and a few of Todd's other sweaty friends flirting with a few women walking past.

"We haven't seen each other in years. It seems like this type of reunion conversation should take place somewhere other than a Subway Shop. Besides, I think your friends are going to get arrested for harassment," I said to Todd and then pointed at Bubba who was on one knee as he held some woman's hand. "Bubba looks like he's proposing to that poor woman."

Bubba wasn't alone. Shakey was putting on a dribbling show with the basketball.

"Who is the skinny one with the basketball?" I asked.

"That's Shakey."

"Why do y'all call him Shakey?"

"I actually met Shakey while I was in the army."

"You went into the army?"

"Yeah girl, a lot has happened since we last saw each other. We got a lot of catching up to do. Anyway, to answer your question, we started calling him Shakey in the army. He used to take showers and then get out of the shower soaking wet. He didn't use towels to dry off."

"Why not?"

"Because he said he liked to air dry. That boy used to walk around in pajamas shaking like a leaf on a tree while he air dried. He would have goose bumps on his arm, but he refused to grab a towel. So we started calling him Shakey.

"We both got out of the army around the same time. It just so happens he was born and raised in the Stone

Mountain area. When I moved to Atlanta we hooked up and kept the friendship going."

"Who is the one moving like a break dancer or something? Oh my goodness, he's doing the moonwalk!"

"That's my boy, Compulsive."

"I'm scared to ask, but I will. Why do y'all call him Compulsive?"

"Because he's always lying. He's actually one of the regular comedians at the club I work at. His whole act is about lying. He'll walk on stage and say something like, 'I was hanging out with Michael Jordan last night' and then the crowd will shout, 'Stop lying' and then he'll tell the truth about what he was really doing the previous night!"

"Is *Compulsive* his stage name?"

"Yes. We started calling him Compulsive because he would lie to us about the silliest things. I guess he liked the name because he eventually made it his stage name, and then developed his entire act around the name.

I chuckled as I marveled at their disregard for public humiliation. "Your friend's aren't afraid of embarrassing themselves?"

"Nah, they could care less. All they want is those chicks' phone numbers to add to their booty call list."

"Compulsive's actually very funny. His popularity is growing here in Atlanta. I think he's close to getting on Def Comedy Jam."

"What is he doing out there?" I asked as I watched Compulsive open a tablet.

"I don't know what he's tellin' that woman. Whatever he's sayin' I know it's a lie because that's the folder I write in. He's probably tellin' her he's a writer or somethin'," Todd replied as he shook his head. Even he had to laugh at the display of buffoonery. "I can't take those fools anywhere."

Eventually Todd refocused on me. "You are right, Sis. This isn't the time or place for this type of catchin' up. Write down my phone number and call me tonight or tomorrow."

I wrote down my brother's phone number. We embraced one last time, and then parted ways. Just as Todd was about to close the door he turned around and said, "It was good to see you, Big Sister."

"It's good to see you too…Todd."

I sat in that same spot for nearly fifteen minutes as I contemplated discarding my brother's phone number. My feelings were scattered. On one hand I was happy to have seen him. On the other hand I wished I'd followed my first inkling and gone to Burger King.

This city has over five million people in it, and dozens of suburbs, what are the odds that I'd run into Todd—in a Subway of all places.

As I sat there processing the entire encounter, an older lady approached me. She had silver hair and looked like one of the women from the old television show, *Golden Girls.*

"I couldn't help, but overhear what you and your brother were talking about," said the woman.

I was startled by her remark. "Excuse me?"

"I'm sorry, I wasn't trying to pry, but I was sitting right here eating and I couldn't help but witness what happened. I lost my brother a few months ago. He was one of my closest friends. He and I used to meet in this store every Monday and eat lunch together. I would give anything to talk to him. You runnin' into your brother is a blessing. Congratulations."

"Thank you," I replied as I watched the fragile-looking woman walk out of the store. I looked upwards towards the ceiling and mumbled, "I get it, God… I'll call him."

8

Rachel

I was in no mood for small talk as I paced around my kitchen with my cell phone pressed against my ear. This was my third attempt at reaching my attorney. I'd called his office earlier that day attempting to reach him, but his assistant claimed he was in depositions all day. I wasn't trying to hear that. I paid him the type of money that dictated he should find some time during the course of his busy day to call back.

Much to my chagrin, it was now well after normal business hours and no one was around to answer his office phone. The moment the beep sounded on his voice mail indicating that a message could be left, I unleashed my fury.

"Lance, this is Rachel! I have been trying to reach you all day and your assistant kept saying you were in a deposition. Now, I don't know if she was lying, but I do know that your ass wasn't busy the entire day. Surely you had five free minutes that you could have used to call me. I will not tolerate being dismissed or blown off. I need you to call me ASAP!"

I could feel my nostrils flaring. I hung up the phone and then went into my bedroom to change my clothes. I reemerged a few minutes later wearing a pair of sweat pants, a large t-shirt, and socks.

"Cupcake, come here!"

"Yes, Ma'am!"

Cupcake is a chubby little girl. Her complexion was lighter than mine and her hair thick and wavy. Some would say that her disposition was much more pleasant than mine. Personally, I believe the child is just a little too carefree. She has a sort of *flower child* attitude that drives me nuts.

Cupcake is the type of child that would smile and wave at the most destitute looking stranger. I always had to stop her from talking to homeless people when we come out of the gas station or some other public place. She's waving and smiling at them while I'm telling them to quit begging and go get a damn job.

That's just one way that my child and I are different. I'm trying to work on her little weight issue; I hope it's just baby fat. Her grades are good, but she's just a little hyper-active in class. I'm working on fixing that too.

After struggling to catch her breath, Cupcake walked down the stairs and entered into the living room area where I sat.

I glanced up at her for just a moment as she approached and then continued to flip through the pages of the magazine I was reading.

"Haven't I told you in the past to stop jumping up and down on that bed?"

"Yes, Ma'am."

"What did I tell you I was going to do to you if I caught you bouncing in that bed again?"

"Punish me."

"Umm hmm. Go get that bag of rice out of the pantry and bring it to me."

Cupcake walked over to the refrigerator and retrieved the rice. Her little eyelids filled with water as she walked slowly with the bag. Clearly in no rush to bring the bag to me, the child walked slowly like a person holding a ticking bomb.

Cupcake knew I didn't play games with her—when I told her to do something I meant it. So, she grew familiar and eventually leery of my punishments. You'd think that would've caused her to stop acting wild, but it didn't. Cupcake is the type of child who needs strict discipline in her life or else she will be out of control.

"I won't do it again, Mommy—I promise." Cupcake tried to talk her way out of the punishment that was quickly approaching.

"I know you won't do it again," I told her as I snatched the bag from her hand.

I stood and walked across the hard wood floor. I stuck my hand in the bag and grabbed a hand full of rice. The uncooked rice was hard like little beads. I sprinkled the rice on the floor in the corner; allowing the rice to fall from my hand like a gardener spreading seeds on fresh soil.

"Come here Cupcake!"

By this time, Cupcake was balling uncontrollably.

"Shut up!" I shouted and then grabbed the child's collar. "You know what to do, so get to it."

Cupcake stopped in a far corner. She was frozen with fear.

"If I have to tell you again, I'm going to make you sleep on the floor. Is that what you want?"

"No, Ma'am."

"Well assume the position!" I shouted.

Cupcake reluctantly kneeled down on the rice. Within seconds her face became distorted and she started to cry. But that fake crying didn't affect me. She knew that no matter how much she performed I wasn't going to let her get up from that position for at least twenty minutes.

When I finally allowed her to stand up she was no longer crying—just making crazy faces. The rice beads were planted into her knee caps. After I plucked all of the beads out of her skin, I took a wet towel and rubbed until the indentations went away. I know some people may think I'm mean, but I see nothing wrong with a little discipline. My grandmother used to make me kneel on uncooked rice when I was being unruly. As a matter of fact, my grandmother used to make me kneel on old Coca-Cola bottle tops. They hurt a hell of a lot more than a few grains if uncooked rice.

I spent the next hour or so helping Cupcake with her homework, and then fixed her some dinner. After we sat down and ate together I prepared her for bed. Just as I finished tucking Cupcake into bed and exited her bedroom, my phone started ringing. I was able to get to the phone before it went to voice mail.

"Hello."

Hey Rachel, I didn't think you were going to answer. I was just about to leave a message.

"Well, there is no need to leave a message, you got me. Lance, I've been trying to contact you all day. What is the status of the paperwork?

Rachel, you keep stressing about this situation. I told you that everything is under control. I've dealt with the necessary documents and all of the paperwork has been filed. All you need to do is continue to build your new life here in Atlanta, and leave that old life and all that drama in California. You won't lose Cupcake. I've already put my most experienced Private

Investigators on your case, and they have ensured me that you are safe.

I felt relieved as I leaned against the wall holding my phone next to my ear. "I just don't need any more headaches. I just want to be left alone."

I understand Rachel. That's why my guys and I are doing all we can to protect you. You have got to trust me.

"I do trust you Lance; it's just that things have been a little stressful lately."

I understand. Just try to focus more on all of the positive things you have going on in your life. Hey, someone's got a birthday coming up in a few days. Are you ready for the big 4-0?

"I'm about as ready as I'm gonna get. Honestly, I haven't given it much thought. I've been so busy at work."

So, did your new assistant start working yet?

"Yeah, she started working today. I was so busy that I didn't get a chance to meet her. But, I will meet her tomorrow. The first thing I'm gonna do is make it very clear what I expect from her."

Are you still having a little birthday get together?

"Yeah, that's the plan. Megan was supposed to have set it up and then pass the details on to this new girl, Kim. I hope for Kim's sake Megan filled her in on everything because if my party isn't exactly the way I want it, her ass will be working somewhere else—just like Megan."

Damn, you are hard on your staff.

"Whatever! All I know is that this new girl Kim had better not screw this up," I replied and then yawned. "I'm tired so I'm gonna get ready for bed. I'll talk to you soon."

Okay. Good night.

9

Kim

The traffic on I-75 was backed up from Georgia Tech University to south of Turner Baseball Stadium. The palms of my hands became sweaty as I realized that I was going to be late for work on my second day on the job.

I wrestled with the idea of whether or not to call the office and tell Rachel I was going to be a little late. That thought was fleeting as I remembered Lucas' words, *"Make sure you come to work on time."*

Nervous and scared that I was about to commit the cardinal sin of a newly hired employee, I called Lucas for advice.

Boxxmore International.

"Lucas, is that you?"

Yes it is. Who is this?

"It's me, Kim. Rachel Biko's new assistant."

Let me guess, you underestimated the amount of traffic on I-75 and now you are about to be late on your second day on the job.

"Lucas, I need your help. Is Rachel there yet?"

Nope, not yet. Awwwh snap!

"What's wrong?"

Rachel just pulled up.

"Shit!" I blurted out.

Don't worry about it, I got you. Where are you now?

"I'm approaching I-20. I'm right next to the baseball stadium."

Okay. In that traffic you are still a good 20 minutes away. Here is what you do. Take I-20 east and get off at the exit before you get to the Morehouse College exit. When you get off the interstate, I want you to turn right and go down a few blocks. You will see a donut shop on the right side of the street. Go in there and get a dozen jelly donuts.

"What?"

Do you wanna keep your job?

"Yes!"

Then do what I'm telling you to do.

Before I could reply, Lucas had hung up the phone. I yanked my steering wheel and exited onto I-20 East. I nearly had a wreck, but at that moment I didn't care. I wasn't about to lose this job.

Twenty minutes later, I came rushing through the door with a nervous look on my face. I was gasping for breath as perspiration beads sat perched on my brow and in the crease between my eyebrows. One sudden jerk of the head in either direction would have sent a stream of sweat streaming down my nose.

"I made it," I said as I plopped the box of donuts on the security counter.

"Don't worry, I covered for you," replied Lucas with a devilish grin. "Now, have a seat for a second and catch your breath."

"What did she say?"

"I told her you came in real early, and then left to go and get her some jelly donuts. I made it sound like you were real eager to impress her."

"Thanks. I can't believe this happened. I'm never late for work."

"It's all good. Most people misjudge that traffic during their first week on the job. Just make sure you leave about thirty minutes earlier tomorrow."

"Trust me, this won't happen again. Tomorrow I might beat you here," I said as I folded the napkin into a tiny square and then dabbed my forehead.

"Well you are good to go today. I told Rachel that you came in real early, and you were trying to impress her by going to buy donuts before she got in. That's your story; you just need to stick to it."

"Good lookin' out!" I replied and gave Lucas a high five. "Have a donut—on me."

I regained my composure and rode the elevator up to my office - well, my desk that sat outside of Rachel's office. As I approached I noticed Rachel's office door partially open. I could see Rachel pacing back and forth. She was wearing a headset as she spoke to someone on the phone.

"I expect you to back off and leave me the hell alone," said Rachel in a terse tone. "Trust me, if you push me I will make your fucking life miserable. Now, I suggest you take that settlement and get lost!"

I figured that if I could hear Rachel's conversation other people in the office could hear it too. I tried to tiptoe and close Rachel's door, but as soon as I touched the door knob Rachel turned around.

"Why are you eavesdropping on my phone call?" Rachel asked me in a very harsh tone.

"I—I was just closing your door." I replied nervously.

I stood in the doorway with my hand glued to the doorknob. Rachel gave me a mean glare. The two of us stared at each other for nearly ten seconds without saying a word. We looked like two cowboys standing in the middle of an old western town preparing for a gunfight. Our eyes were our six shooters. The first person who blinked was the loser.

I fought hard to keep my knees from knocking. Rachel's glare was intense. She would have made the average first day employee wilt. It may have been my first day of work, but I was far from weak. I may have deliberately stored away much of my New Orleans memories, but the one lesson I did recall from my hometown was that even if you are intimidated, you never let the other person see it.

I believe that awkward moment served as somewhat of a positive ice breaker for Rachel and me. I can tell she was surprised that I didn't blink or scurry away.

"I have to go," Rachel said to whomever she was talking to on the phone, and then clicked the button to turn off her headset.

"Well, are you gonna stand in my doorway or are you coming in?"

I let out a silent sigh as I stepped in Rachel's office. I remembered that my alibi for not being there when Rachel arrived was the donuts, so I quickly grabbed the box and then walked in to formally introduce myself.

"I'm sorry for the misunderstanding Rachel—I mean Ms. Biko. I would never try to eavesdrop on your conversation. I noticed one of the other executives in the hallway, and I didn't want him to hear your conversation."

Rachel stood there silently as she continued to size me up.

"Umm, we haven't formally met. My name is..."

"I know that your name is Kim," Rachel interjected. "I guess you are probably wondering why I didn't interview you."

"Actually, I was curious why you allowed the person whom I replaced to do the entire interview process."

Rachel sat at her desk and then reclined in her huge black leather chair. "I let Megan do it for two reasons. The first reason is obvious—I was too busy to do it myself. Secondly, I will be able to tell within 48 hours whether or not you can handle the job. If I end up releasing you within that time frame then I would have avoided wasting my own time during the interview process."

Rachel was blunt and direct, but I wasn't bothered by her tone. As a matter of fact, I immediately felt sorry for Rachel. It was clear to see that Rachel had an awesome job, and was blessed in many ways. I figured that anyone who could be this grouchy at nine o'clock with no provocation must really be hurting inside. I know a lot about pain.

She's trying too hard. This sista is obviously stressed out. I'm just gonna do my job and watch her back. She needs an ally. I'm sure she doesn't believe she needs one, but she does. That person will be me.

I cleared my throat and then put on my game face.

"I know that you are real busy today, Ms. Biko. So, I'm going to say what I need to say and get out of your way. You have an eleven o'clock phone conference with the Vice President of Operations at Siemens. I've already gathered up the monthly reports from all the Directors and prepared a rough draft quarterly report for you to look over. I sent it as an email attachment. You can tell me what you like and don't like about it—I'll change it accordingly. Your daughter's dance class has been rescheduled for tomorrow evening. Last but not least, I'm almost finished coordinating your birthday celebration, I'm just waiting to hear back from the musician that will be playing at the event. As soon as I take care of that I will have the invitations completed and sent out."

Rachel was speechless. Her facial expression went from menacing and frustrated to pleased—even somewhat relieved. I was hoping she viewed me as a younger version of herself.

"Do you need me to do anything else right now?" I asked, confidant that I'd just made a good first impression—minus the little snafu at the door a few moments earlier.

"That will be all," Rachel replied.

I immediately turned and walked out of the door. I didn't look back, but I could feel Rachel's glaring eyes fixated on my back.

"Uhh, Kim," Rachel called out.

Shit! I knew she was gonna have something to say. "Yes, Ms. Biko," I replied as I stopped at the doorway, and then turned slowly to face my new boss.

"Call me Rachel," Rachel said without looking up at me.

"Yes, Ms. Biko—I mean, Rachel."

I closed Rachel's office door and then went straight into the ladies restroom down the hall. I stepped into a stall, put my head between my legs, and then prayed quietly as I fought back a scream of joy.

Thank you Lord. Thank you.

10

Rachel

She didn't blink when I stared her down. She seems to care about her appearance. She seems intelligent. She already knows what kind of donuts I like. Most importantly, she's already trying to protect me more than Megan's no-good ass did.

I had so much stuff on my mind after that phone call that I wanted to leave work right then. Most of the other Vice President's around there would have taken the rest of the week off after returning from Europe, but I didn't feel like I had that luxury. I'm an African-American woman in an all white corporate environment. Taking days off to recoup from traveling isn't an option.

Besides, I needed to meet Kim. She was going to be my gate keeper and I needed to see where her head was as soon as possible. I made the mistake of trusting Megan too soon, and she screwed me big time.

The remainder of the day went relatively fast. My meetings were hick-up free. I was able to give the C.E.O. the information he'd been requesting—thanks to some research by Kim. I even had time to enjoy the jelly donuts Kim brought in.

Around three o'clock I decided to shut it down. As I walked past Kim's desk I noticed that it was neat and organized—I liked that.

"A clean desk is a sign of someone with good organizational skills," I said to Kim.

She looked startled. My comment caught her off guard. I suspect Megan - and probably Lucas - told her that I was some type of tyrant.

"Umm, I guess you can call it tidy. I hate a cluttered desk—that's kind of a pet peeve of mine."

Good reply. Based on her attitude and her performance today, this girl may have a chance to make it around here.

"So, what are you doing after work?"

"Excuse me?"

"What are your plans after you leave here today?"

"Ummm, nothing really. I was going to go home and watch some soap operas I recorded," Kim replied, clearly confused by my question.

"I'm kind of hungry. I think I'm gonna go and grab a bite to eat. Would you like to join me? I'm paying."

"Sure!" Kim replied excitedly.

Kim turned off her computer and we headed out the door. I was really hungry and dying to have a nice meal, but I did have a hidden agenda. The real reason why I invited Kim to dinner was so that I could pick her brains away from the office.

Because of my personal issues, it wasn't good enough for a person to work as my assistant and not be privy to some of my personal life. My job required me to do so much traveling that the person working as my assistant would have access to my computer, mail, and maybe even my spare house keys. I needed to make sure this girl was up to the task.

As we were leaving the building Kim said she needed to use the restroom. I told her to meet me at my car because I needed to make a phone call. I sat in my car and used my new cellular phone to call Lucas. He was wrapping up the final details on a very important personal matter of mine. Kim's momentary departure was perfect. The topic of me and Lucas' conversation was highly sensitive.

11

Kim

As I walked out the front entrance to the building the first thing I noticed was the tires on Rachel's Jaguar. They were so shiny they looked wet.

Rachel was already sitting in the car waiting for me. She was talking on her cell phone, and based on the expression on her face, the conversation was rather intense.

At first I was going to stand outside and wait until she finished her conversation, but it didn't seem like she was going to wrap it up anytime soon. As I approached the car I heard the front door unlock so I opened the door. When I slid onto the plush leather seats of the fine automobile I felt like I wanted to faint.

Shit I think I'm about to have an orgasm. Oh my goodness, these are the softest seats I've ever felt in my life. Look at the wood grain on the dashboard. This thing looks like a damn spaceship.

I slowly turned and looked over my shoulder. I moved so slow and deliberate that you would have thought the boogey man was sitting behind me preparing to get me.

The back seat looks better than that fake leather sofa I have in my apartment. Damn, even the carpet in here is better than the carpet in my apartment. Shit, I should ask Rachel if I can just break my lease and move into her car. This is what I want.

I have got to position myself so that I can have the finer things in life—stuff like this car—and those damn BCBG shoes that heifer's wearing. She ain't even rocking those shoes the way I would. It drives me crazy to see people with money not know what to do with it.

I wish, I wish....awwh shit, I think these car seats are vibrating. Damn, they're massaging my ass! Oooooh. Ooooohwee. Thiiiiis shiiiit feeeeels soooo gooooooood.

My silent freak-fest with the car seats was interrupted when Rachel started shouting on the phone.

"Lance, I don't care what you do to fix this. I just want that part of my life to be over with. I don't ever want to hear the name Lecar again. I can take care of my child—I don't need any help. I can take care of my career—I don't need any help with that. I just need you to do what I've asked you to do. The next time we talk I want you to be able to tell me some good news."

Rachel hung up the phone and then let out a sigh. She smacked the steering wheel and then looked up at the ceiling.

"Are you okay?" I asked.

Rachel didn't respond. She put the car gear in reverse, looked over her right shoulder, and then backed out of the space. Silence prevailed for the first five minutes of the drive. My emotional intelligence kicked in and alerted me that Rachel needed some time to decompress.

"Do you like sushi?" asked Rachel.

Hell no I don't like sushi! Why would I want to eat raw fish? I'm a human not a bear. I don't normally eat sushi, but you had better believe I was gonna eat it that day.

"I love sushi," I said, lying with a straight face.

"Good. I know the perfect spot a few blocks from here. It's actually a steak and sushi restaurant."

We arrived at the restaurant and immediately seated. Rachel seemed at home and comfortable while I sat there looking like a fish out of water—no pun intended. I'd never held a pair of chopsticks and I definitely didn't know what to order. I was gonna order a steak, but before I could decide what to order Rachel put me on the spot.

"So what do you like?" asked Rachel.

"Ummm, ummm," I stuttered. "Oooh, I see so much good stuff on here, I don't know what to order. This ginger looks good. What do you normally get?"

"I like the Crispy Shrimp Roll and Tuna Roll."

"That sounds good," I said as I stared at the menu. "I'll just get whatever you are getting."

Rachel looked at me and then placed her menu on the table. "Kim, you don't have any idea what to order do you?"

I put down the menu and then shook my head—too ashamed to look into Rachel's eyes.

Rachel chuckled. "I knew you didn't."

"What did I do to tip you off?"

"Anyone who has eaten sushi before knows that the Ginger is just a side item designed to enhance the flavor. You made it sound like it was something you could actually order."

We both burst into laughter. I was busted. Fortunately for me, Rachel got a kick out of my ignorance.

"I'll order you some Spicy California Rolls. That's good for beginners, plus it has a little spice on it so you should like it. Y'all Louisianans like your food spicy."

"Yes we do—real spicy."

When the waiter came over to our table Rachel ordered our food.

"Excuse me, I'm gonna run to the restroom," said Rachel and then got up.

"Okay."

I should have ordered a piece of steak instead of letting Rachel pressure me into ordering this sushi. I hope I don't throw up.

12

Rachel

I decided that I would wait until after we ate dinner before I hit Kim with the real hard questions. As I was leaving out of the restroom I passed in front of the bar. Out of my peripheral vision I noticed the oddest thing—a black bartender in an Asian owned restaurant.

My intent was to hurry up back to my table so that I could get ready to eat my food, but something about this man caught my eye. He had long dreadlocks that were pulled back like a ponytail. If it wasn't for the thick band securing them they would have flown like the mane of a lion.

Damn he's fine. I don't usually go for the dreadlock look, but he is cute—almost exotic looking.

When I got back to the table I tried to focus on my conversation with Kim, but I couldn't help but glance over at that bartender every few seconds. I guess my attempts to be discreet with my peeking were ineffective because Kim figured out what was going on.

"Is everything okay?" Kim asked.

I pretended I didn't know what she was talking about. "Yeah, why do you ask?"

"I just notice that you keep glancing over towards the bar. Are you sure everything's okay?"

"Ummm yeah," I replied initially, but for some reason I felt comfortable enough with Kim that I finally confessed. "Actually, I'm glancing over there because that bartender is cute."

"What bartender?"

"That guy over there—with the dreadlocks. He's kinda cute. I've been here a couple of times, but I've never seen him in here."

Kim looked over at the bartender and then quickly turned her head. I guess she didn't think he was that cute. Fine by me, I don't need her trying to make a move on him first. He was mine. I was just hoping he'd look over at us so that I could make eye contact.

When our food came I didn't bother looking up at that bartender again. I pulled out a pair of chopsticks and started digging in. Poor Kim was catching hell trying to pick up that sushi with those chopsticks.

"So what do you think?" I asked.

"Think about what?"

"The bartender; did you see him?"

"Oh yeah, I saw him."'

"Well, what do you think? Do you think he's cute?"

"Yeah he's handsome," she replied nonchalantly. "He doesn't look like your type."

What in the hell does that mean? He looks like he's in his late twenties. Does she think I'm too old for him? Is she implying that he's more her speed? I know she's not suggesting that, because I look better than she does.

"What do you mean by that?"

"I mean, when I look at you I don't see you with a guy wearing dreadlocks. Based on your appearance and your job, I would assume that you would be with a white collar guy—not a dreadlock wearing bartender. That's just my opinion."

"Fair enough. Those white collar men I come in contact with are too stuffy and uptight. Besides, there aren't many available black men in the corporate world."

"I guess you're right," Kim replied. "I haven't been in this environment long enough to really comment on that."

"Trust me when I tell you, there aren't many brothas roaming the halls in my world. I'm usually the only black person in the room—man or woman."

I glanced at the bar again and damn near choked on my sushi when I noticed that dreadlock Adonis staring at me.

"What's wrong?" Kim asked when she noticed me hustling to wipe the soy sauce from my chin.

"He's looking over here."

"Who?"

I had to look at her for a moment like she was crazy. "Who do you think? Who have I been talking about? The bartender; he just smiled at me and winked."

Kim seemed disinterested. If I didn't know any better I'd think she was hating on me. Maybe she was jealous that he wasn't flirting with her.

As I sat there trying to assess Kim's attitude I got the shock of my life—Mr. Dreadlocks started coming towards our table.

13

Kim

Ain't this a bitch! Of all the restaurants in the city of Atlanta, we end up in the place Todd is working at. I swear; it's like he has a damn tracking device on me. I'd forgotten he told me he had a part-time job at a restaurant. Just my luck, it would be this one. To make matters worse, my new boss is sitting here drooling over him.

I tried to ignore Rachel at first and pretend like I didn't see him, but the truth of the matter is, I instinctively knew who she was talking about the moment she used the words *bartender* and *dreadlocks*.

When I finally looked over and saw my little brother at that bar I wanted to hide under the table. He was in fact as handsome as she described, but I wasn't about to comment on his looks because I knew that would spark the type of conversation that would be both uncomfortable and extensive.

I was about to make an excuse for us to get out of there and maybe tell her I had to go home and feed my dog and cat. Any type of lame excuse would have sufficed. I just needed to get out of there before Todd noticed me.

Sometimes I feel like God likes to have a chuckle at my expense because it seems like He loves watching me squirm. Just when I thought my luck couldn't get any worse, it did. I looked up from that plate of raw fish and rice and guess who was standing at our table? Yep, you guessed it. My brother Todd.

"What's up, Big Sis!" said Todd exuberantly.

"Todd! Hey!" I replied and then stood up to hug him.

"You two know each other?" Rachel asked. She had a jealous look on her face. I guess she figured I was about to steal the object of her desire. At that point I had no choice, but to introduce to them.

"This is my little brother, Todd," I said reluctantly. "Todd, this is Rachel."

"Your *little brother?*" asked Rachel rhetorically as she stuck out her hand to shake Todd's. "I didn't know you had a brother."

How could you, you haven't talked to me for more than five straight minutes since I started working for you.

"Yeah, we haven't seen each other in years," I said.

Todd's gaze at Rachel was just as intense. It was clear to anyone paying attention that I was going to be dismissed by either or both of them real soon.

"I'm Todd," he said as he gently clinched Rachel's perfectly manicured fingers—deliberately rubbing his thumb across her knuckles as he shook her hand.

"Rachel," she replied in a voice that was so flirtatious it made me do a double take. "I'm your sister's new boss."

"Oh really? I always said she was the lucky one in the family."

I thought I was going to puke as I watched my brother and boss undress each other with their eyes.

"So, y'all in here getting' y'all sushi on. Kim I didn't know you ate sushi. When we were kids you didn't even eat fish—fried or grilled."

I know he ain't trying to crack on me. When we were kids Todd always tried to embarrass me, but I'm not about to let him make me the butt of a joke in front of Rachel.

"Well Todd, we haven't been around each other in years. There are a lot of things you don't know about me."

"I've never seen you in here," said Rachel.

"I've been working here for a few months, Ms Rachel…" Todd replied.

"Biko. Rachel Biko."

"Rachel Biko…that's sexy. I've never seen you here either."

Oh God, I think I'm gonna puke. I felt like the woman in the bubble bath commercial—*Calgon take me away!*

"Your sister and I are just getting better acquainted. We still have to talk about some stuff—mainly my party," said Rachel and then looked at me and smiled.

"So you're having a party," Todd replied.

I immediately started to cringe when I heard his comment. I know my brother. When we were kids he and his friends used to ride around looking for parties to crash. I'm sure he hasn't changed. Besides, I'd just met his current batch of friends, and there was no way in hell I wanted any of them at a party I was affiliated with.

"Well, I'm still wrapping up the final arrangements for the party. That reminds me, I'm still waiting to hear back from a musician, but he hasn't called."

"A musician?" asked Todd.

"Yeah, there is going to be a band performing and the band leader was supposed to call me today."

"When is the party?"

"This weekend," Rachel replied.

"Where is it gonna be?" Todd asked.

"At the Jaguar dealership on Peachtree," I replied hesitantly.

"Yeah, that's the big thing now days," said Todd. "I know someone who gave a party at the Cadillac dealership. It was nice."

"If you are pressed for time, and the musician you've been waiting on hasn't called you back, you could probably book the band that works at the nightclub where I work."

I wanted to decline Todd's recommendation, but I didn't feel like I had that luxury. Besides, I didn't think it would look good to blow him off in front of Rachel. The fact of the matter was, my Plan A wasn't coming through; I needed a Plan B.

"What kind of music do they play?" I asked.

"You name it, they play it. R&B, Jazz, Hip-Hop – you name it they play it," Todd replied. "If you are still waiting on that first band to call you back this late in the game, then you are playing with fire."

"You've got a point," said Rachel.

"How about this – I will be at the club doing inventory tomorrow afternoon; come and check out the band while they practice. I know for a fact that they've been looking for some gigs. I'll bet they are cheaper than that band you were going to use. I'll even introduce you to the band leader."

"You should come to the party, Todd." Rachel suggested.

Shit. I knew this was going to happen.

"Really," Todd replied.

By this time, Rachel was in full drool mode. She was practically throwing the coochie at Todd.

"Sure. You should come," Rachel reiterated.

"Cool. Can I bring a few of my buddies?"

Please say no Rachel. Trust me, you don't want those ghetto ass-niggas at your party.

"That's fine. The more the merrier. We're gonna have lots of food and drinks."

"Great. Kim, call me when you are on your way to the club to check out the band. "

Rachel and I left the restaurant and drove back to the office. That was the longest 15 minute ride of my life. You would have thought she'd just met Michael Jordan the way she went on and on about Todd. I came dangerously close to telling her to shut the hell up. But, the prospect of being instantly unemployed was enough to control my razor sharp tongue. Instead I sat there in that car and wished I'd saved some of those damn jelly donuts and eaten them for dinner instead.

14

Kim

There was a buzz in the showroom – the type of synergy created at events where most of the guests want to be seen and heard. It was a very diverse crowd. Most of the black folk in attendance all seemed to have an air of pretentiousness about them.

Clean-shaven pompous looking men sipped on dark colored drinks in bourbon glasses while spouting their resumes to sophisticated black women sipping on colorful drinks in martini glasses. Not to be outdone by the self absorbed men vying for their attention, the women in attendance seemed just as eager to tout their own accomplishments.

The people may have been a little stuffy, but the venue was awesome. All styles of Jaguar vehicles littered the massive showroom floor while several waiters holding trays made their way in and out of small pockets of people as they effectively ensured that the guests kept hors d'oeuvres in their hands along with replenished drinks.

A saxophonist walked around the room playing seductive tunes. The allure of sex dripped from every intoxicating note he played. There were several millionaires and a ton of wannabes there boasting and bragging.

In one corner of the room was a football player for the Atlanta Falcons eyeballing the newest Jaguar. While he discussed the car with one of the executives from Boxxmore—a self-proclaimed Jaguar expert—three, 30 plus year old groupies stood on the side snickering as they sipped on their martinis and stared at his ass.

Athletes weren't the only people in attendance. On the other side of the room was Jerry Jacobs, a millionaire real estate investor. He stood there arguing sports with Dr. Heller, a brain surgeon. Cole Hide, the highest ranking executive at Boxxmore was posted in the corner with a woman who wasn't his wife. The mood was definitely ripe for everyone to have a good time.

Everything seemed to be going exactly the way I envisioned, but there was one thing missing—the guest of honor. The party was scheduled to start at nine. The clock was quickly approaching 10 p.m. and Rachel was nowhere to be found.

Maybe I should call and see where she is, I thought to myself. The desire to check on my boss was a fleeting one. No sooner than the thought crossed my mind a second voice that was snuggled in my subconscious mind blurted out, *Bitch are you crazy? Rachel will embarrass you in front of all these people if she even thinks you are trying to keep tabs on her. Divas show up late to parties, and Rachel is the biggest diva you know.*

"I'm just gonna make sure these people stay liquored up so that they won't notice that Rachel hasn't arrived yet," I mumbled.

As I stood near the center of the showroom pointing out a spilled drink to a member of the cleaning crew, I heard another drink smash on the floor.

"Oh, my bad, Dog," barked a deep husky voice.

"Oh shit," I mumbled as I looked towards the entrance and saw that the apology came from none other than Big Bubba. He'd inadvertently bumped into one of those pretentious guys who'd been bragging about his career since he got there.

The arrogant man spilled his drink all over his own blazer and then dropped the glass to the floor. He cursed out loud and was about to yell at Big Bubba until he saw that Bubba stood six inches taller than he did and easily outweighed him by 200 lbs.

Compulsive came in behind Bubba. He had barely placed his feet onto the showroom floor and he was already lying to a group of women as he passed out business cards. It was unclear what type of title he had on the cards, but I could hear him telling the women to ignore the scratched out phone numbers on the front.

"Don't worry about that number right there, that's my old phone number. My updated contact info can be found on the back of the card," said Compulsive as he attempted to sneak a peek at their cleavage.

"Why is your information written in ink?" asked one of the women.

"Oh, that's because these are my old cards. I got two promotions at my job since these were made about two months ago. They gave me a corner office with a new phone number. I got some new business cards coming, but for now

I just wrote down the info. Don't worry about that stuff on the front just check out the back."

"So what do you do at your company?" asked one of the women.

"Actually, I have a government job. The shit I do is classified."

"Oh really?" asked one of the women sarcastically.

"Seriously," Compulsive replied defensively. "I got a Double Top Secret Clearance. You gotta be in the Secret Service to have my level of clearance."

"So are you telling us that you're in the Secret Service?'

"Nah, I started to join the Secret Service, but they want you to work nights and shit. I'm a comedian at night, if I had become a Secret Service agent that would have fucked up my night hustle. Besides, at that time old man Bush was still the President. I wasn't trying to take a bullet for his ass."

"So let me get this straight, you have a Top Secret clearance?"

"Actually it's a Triple Top Secret clearance," Compulsive interjected.

"Hold up, you said it was a Double Top Secret clearance a few seconds ago," blurted out one of the women.

"Uhhh, it used to be a Double Top Secret, but when I got promoted they went ahead and moved it up to a Triple."

"Girl he is lying. He got a high ranking government job, but he's a comedian at night. Y'all can sit here and listen to these lies, but I'm going over here where the real movers and shakers are."

"Hold up, booboo. How you gonna question a nigga's governmental classification?" Compulsive replied with an indignant look on his face. "Ya see, that what's wrong with sista's today. Y'all want a brotha to have multiple hustles, but y'all can't handle it when you meet a real hustla. For your information, Boo—I tell jokes at night so that I can have a backup career in case the government thing doesn't work."

"Whatever," replied the three women in unison as they tossed Compulsive's business cards onto a nearby table.

"Why y'all can't respect a nigga's career plans and just support a brotha?"

While Compulsive stood there lying to those women about his phantom job, Shakey started to get his drink on. He flagged down a waiter who was passing by and snatched two drinks off the tray—one for each hand. He looked crazy as hell standing there sipping on two blue drinks with little miniature umbrellas in them.

Todd was the last of the crew to come through the door. He surveyed the room in search of the guest of honor. He then secured an open space by a column and stared at the fancy cars being showcased. After admiring the cars from afar, he made his way near one of the 8 cylinder beauties and caressed the soft interior.

I can't believe he brought his ghetto ass friends up in here. They're gonna embarrass the hell out of me tonight—I just know it.

I tried to turn and walk in a different direction when I saw Todd and his crew. For a moment I stood there and watched my baby brother from afar. He hadn't changed much. A little taller and more muscular, but he was the same Todd.

As Todd moved, his shoulder length dreadlocks swayed with each step he took. I recalled how many of my high school girlfriends would beg me to set them up with him.

Despite Todd's genuine desire to reconnect with me, I was still hesitant to let him back into my life. No matter how hard I tried, I could not move past the deep seated anger I felt for Todd. His assertion ten years earlier that my hesitancy to go get help was the reason our mother died that ill-fated night, was etched into my memory.

I was unable to stop Rachel from inviting Todd to her birthday celebration, but I figured I could control whether or not I socialized with him. I looked towards the floor as I tried to exit out of a side door that led to the restrooms. Unfortunately, I walked right into the stomach of my newest admirer – Big Bubba.

"Hey future wifey!"

"Oh, uhh, hi…Bubba, right?" I asked nervously.

"I told you, you can call me Big Bubbly," replied Bubba as he rubbed his hands together and licked his lips. He was staring at me like I was a pork chop.

"Tee," Bubba shouted as he gestured for Todd to come over. "Look who I found!"

"Hey Kim," Todd shouted as he slid past the small pockets of people.

If I could have made myself disappear I would have, but David Copperfield, I was not. I had to face my biological brother; a brother I felt no kinship towards.

I envisioned myself being cornered all night as Todd tried to force me to answer questions about my whereabouts over the last ten years. I cringed at the thought of being obligated to embrace Todd's desire to reconcile. The fact that Todd expected me to just ignore our past, and get on with our lives as if we'd never feuded was repulsive to me.

I watched my brother maneuver through the crowd. His long dreadlocks lay on his shoulder like strands of tightly woven rope. Uptight corporate types glanced as the dreadlocked king sauntered past. As those *buppies* looked at Todd with disdain, their female dates could be seen peeking with lustful looks in their eyes.

Todd's dreadlocks appeared exotic when seen amongst those uptight Brooks Brother's suit-wearing corporate geeks. His mere presence amongst that white collared group garnered attention—good and bad. But, while everyone else saw a young man who seemed intriguingly different, I saw a person whom I couldn't forgive.

As Todd approached me flashing his award winning smile, I caught flashbacks of my physical fight with him in the psychiatrist's office ten years earlier. That was the last time I'd seen him—I thought it was going to be the very last.

Memories started racing in my head. Disturbing images; images like the night our mother was murdered. It was as if I'd gone through some type of time warp.

My body grew tense. Suddenly Todd appeared to be moving towards me in slow motion as many of the painful remarks he'd made to me resurfaced in her mind.

'If it wasn't for you our mother would still be alive'; 'Don't just stand there, run across the street and go get help!'; 'I wish you would have died instead of mama.'

By the time Todd was standing within three feet of me my eye lids were struggling to hold back the huge puddles of tears that were desperately trying to escape.

"What's up, Kim?" Todd shouted as he gave me a bear hug.

"Hey," I replied and gave Todd one of those fake double pats on the back hugs—the type women in the church give those annoying single men that are always trying to flirt on the low.

"I told you I was gonna come through."

"I see you brought your posse with you."

"Yeah, I try to show them how the big ballas live sometime. Now that my sista is stomping with the big dogs, I figured this would be a good time for me to show off and do a little stunting. You know how it is sis."

I managed a fake smile and pretended to be amused, but deep down I just wanted my space. Just as I was about to come up with an excuse to get away from Todd—and Bubba's annoying ass—I heard another familiar voice.

"Kim, so this is where you've been," commented Rachel as she stood behind me with a peculiar look on her face. I couldn't tell if Rachel was annoyed or just making small talk. "I've been looking for you for the past ten minutes."

"Hey, Rachel," I replied nervously. "I didn't know you were here. I was just trying to entertain the guest until you arrived."

"I was here before the event started. I was just hanging in the background out of site trying to see how you handled a little pressure. I'm impressed. I can see that you are completely comfortable *entertaining* guests," said Rachel as she stared at Todd like he was a piece of prime rib.

"So Kim, do you know what Big Bubba thought about last night?" said Bubba.

I looked at Bubba and tried to come up with a clever line to shut him down before he got started, but I was too slow.

"I'ma tell you what Big Bubba thought about. Big Bubba was wondering if he'd get a chance to dance with pretty Ms. Kim tonight."

Much to my chagrin, the saxophonist stopped playing his horn and the band Todd referred me to, started playing a few modern tunes just as Bubba spoke. A tall busty singer stepped on the makeshift stage and prepared to start singing. The beat to Boyz II Men's hit song, *Motown Philiy*, started playing.

"Awwwh shit, that's the jam right there!" Bubba blurted out.

I immediately panicked. I instinctively knew what was coming next.

No he didn't say, that's the jam. *I gotta lose this big country fool before he decides to ask me to...*

"Cupid is in the house tonight! Come on, Kim. Dance with Big Bubbly."

Before I could say no, Bubba grabbed my hand and led me to the dance floor. Todd chuckled as he watched me be overwhelmed by his buddy's personality.

"Well Boss Lady, are you gonna leave me standing here looking crazy or are you gonna dance with me?" Todd asked Rachel as he smiled flirtatiously.

"I'd like that," Rachel replied, and grabbed Todd's elbow as he escorted her to the dance floor.

The couple commandeered a spot on the dance floor right next to Bubba and me. I looked rigid and timid while Bubba moved his three hundred plus pounds like a Soul Train dancer. Every sway of his humongous hips was accompanied with a sound effect like, "Awwh shit", "Oh yeah", and "Watch out now".

I looked like a woman in one of those commercials where the voice over says, *Wanna get away?*

"C'mon, Kim. Move those sweet hips," said Bubba.

"Yeah, Kim. I know you ain't gonna let Big Bubba out dance you on this dance floor," said Todd, smirking and clearly enjoying instigating this madness.

"You need to be worrying about me out dancing you," said Rachel as she shook her breast in Todd's face to make sure she had his undivided attention.

Todd quickly refocused on the stunning creature standing before him. He gazed deep into Rachel's eyes and then deliberately let her see him survey her breast, hips, and legs. Rachel took his not so subtle hint and then upped the ante. She slowly started rotating her hips, and then turned around so that he could see how much wagon she was dragging.

When Todd seemed hesitant to move in and take control of this opportunity being presented to him, Rachel decided to help him out. She took a step backwards and then pressed her butt cheeks up against Todd's groin. She then reached around and gripped Todd's hips.

Todd couldn't hide his surprise. He looked at Bubba and smiled.

"Yeah, Tee. That's what I'm talkin' 'bout, Boy!" Bubba shouted.

"If this is too grown and sexy for you, let me know," Rachel turned and whispered, taunting Todd just to see how aggressive he would get.

Todd didn't disappoint. He placed his hands on Rachel's and started grinding on her so hard that she could feel his manhood grow and lodge between her butt crack along with the laced thong she wore.

"Don't play with me... I'm a grown-ass man," he whispered in Rachel's ear.

"I can feel that," Rachel replied.

I thought I was going to hyperventilate as I watched my boss dirty dance with my brother less than three feet away from me. While I was focusing on Todd and Rachel gyrate like they were the only two people in the room, Bubba made his move.

Bubba must have been inspired by Todd's actions because he started licking his lips. At first I thought he envisioned me being a steak or a piece of chicken like the characters used to do in the old Tom and Jerry cartoons, but I realized that he wasn't hungry—just horny.

"Awwwwh shit," Bubba mumbled as he slipped behind me and pressed his body up against mine.

"Bubba, if you don't get yo big ass off of me..." I shouted and then pushed Bubba. He was so big that he didn't budge.

I was so annoyed at him that I just turned and walked away—leaving him on the dance floor.

"Damn, Kim., You gonna leave Big Bubba on this floor all alone?" Bubba shouted.

I didn't even look back as I walked off the floor. I made it to the female bathroom within seconds. I opened the door of the nearest stall and sat down on the toilet seat. I didn't have to use the toilet; I just needed a little solitude so that I could digest everything that was happening. My thoughts were all over the place.

I don't believe this is happening. Todd and his friends have got to get out of here. Better yet, they need to get out of my life. And what was that with him and Rachel? She was throwing herself on him. Huh, Christian my ass! She damn near offered him the pussy right there on the dance floor.

My moment of silence was interrupted by a pair of women that entered the restroom. I could not see them, but I could hear their conversation.

"Girl, did you see Ms. Biko on that dance floor bumping and grinding with that dude with the dreadlocks," said the first high pitched voice.

"I sure did. She walks around the office acting all high maintenance and stuck up, but she's sure looking freaky out there. I guess we know who she's going home with tonight," replied the second woman in a sarcastic tone.

The women spent a few seconds in the restroom commenting on other people at the party, and then left out. It's unclear if they even realized I was in there, but I definitely heard them.

"This isn't good," I mumbled. "Those heifers are going to spread all kinds of rumors about Rachel."

I left the stall and rejoined the party. I wanted to let Rachel know what I'd overheard the women say. My job was to support and look out for Rachel, and that's what I intended to do.

The dance floor was packed as the singer belted out a pretty good version of Michael Jackson's, *Another Part of Me*. I could see Bubba on the dance floor with two women.

Shakey was in the corner talking to an unidentified woman. He had a wine glass in one hand and a mixed drink in the other as he leaned up against the wall trying to whisper in her ear while she looked totally disinterested in what he was saying.

Standing less than ten feet away from Shakey was Compulsive. Compulsive was talking to Jim Nash, the President of Boxxmore International. I wasn't sure what he was telling Mr. Nash, but I figured it was a lie because I could see Compulsive displaying those homemade business cards. He was turning the card over and pointing to the writing on it.

"Lawd have mercy, what is Compulsive doing?" I mumbled nervously. "There ain't no telling what he is over there saying to Mr. Nash."

I walked over to Compulsive hoping and praying that the lie he was telling was at least partially believable. As I got within earshot I realized that my worst fear was actually coming to life.

"Yeah, I used to date Jada way before she met Will," Compulsive said in a very confidant tone.

"Are you serious?" asked Mr. Nash. I couldn't tell if he was actually buying the bullshit Compulsive was selling, but the look on that man's face suggested that he was.

"I had to break up with her because she was a little too jealous for me. She couldn't handle my success. That's when she started dating Will Smith. He was still on that show *Fresh Prince of Bel Air* at that time. He was a nice boy—that's the kinda dude she needed back then. I was too wild for her. She wanted to tame a brotha and I wasn't tryin' to have that. During that time I was on tour with Eddie."

"Eddie?" asked Mr. Nash.

"Yeah Eddie... Eddie Murphy," Compulsive replied in a tone that suggested he was annoyed at the fact that he had to explain which Eddie he was referring to.

"You know Eddie? You don't look old enough to have hung out with him."

"Hell yeah I know Eddie! I knew Eddie back when…"

"There you are," I interrupted. I was determined to stop Compulsive's lying. I didn't know his real name, and I didn't want to call him Compulsive in front of Mr. Nash, so I pretended to be looking for him. "I've been looking for you. Let's dance."

"Heeeeey," Compulsive replied, clearly surprised by my presence. He turned to Mr. Nash and smirked. "Look here Jim baby; I'ma have to get with you later dog. I gotta give this honey what she wants or else she's gonna be botherin' a brotha all night."

Mr. Nash, clearly buzzing from the whiskey he was sipping, raised his drink in approval and then gave Compulsive a wink and a high five.

I rolled my eyes, gave Compulsive a *nigga please* look, and then led him to the dance floor. Once we got on the floor I revealed the real reason I asked him to dance.

"Have you seen my brother?"

"Huh?"

"Todd. Have you seen my brother, Todd?"

"Oh yeah. You are Tee's sister. I'm so fucked up I didn't even recognize you."

"Yeah, I know. Have you seen Todd?"

"The last time I saw him he was heading outside with some chick."

"What did she look like?"

"She looked a little older than him; like she was pushing forty. I don't know how old she was, but she was finer than a ma'fucka!"

"This is *her* party," I said, ticked off at the fact that Compulsive was at an event getting drunk and telling lies, and didn't even know who or what the event was for.

"Yeeeeah, that's what I'm talkin' bout! Tee comes to the event and automatically lands the biggest fish."

"Yeah, yeah, whatever," I replied, and then walked away, leaving Compulsive on the dance floor looking lost.

Outside, the sky was so clear that it made the stars look like a million tiny light bulbs suspended in mid-air. The temperature was a mild 72 degrees—perfect weather for getting your *mack* on.

Located at the end of the sidewalk was a silver Jaguar. Sitting on the hood of the car was Rachel. Todd was leaning against the door and driver side windshield as he talked to her. All I could see as I approached the two of them was Todd's hands gesture back and forward while he spoke and Rachel flashing a smile that was brighter than the aforementioned stars dangling above our heads.

When I got about ten feet away I saw Todd pull out his cell phone and start pressing the numbers. I slowed my pace as I marveled at what I was witnessing.

"I don't believe this shit," I mumbled in a tone loud enough that only I could hear. "She is giving him her phone number. How can he just show up after all these years and force his way back into my life? Oh hell no, this isn't about to happen—not if I can help it."

Determined to derail any romantic momentum that may have been building between Rachel and Todd, I put on my big sister *hater* cape and swooped in.

"Look at y'all out here hiding like two high school kids," I said in a playful tone. "Todd get away from my boss, she doesn't want to be bothered with your crazy butt. Besides, you're gonna
lose that number by the time you get to work at that bar this weekend. You know you're going to be distracted by all those hoochies running around."

Todd stopped what he was doing and looked at me in bewilderment. He couldn't believe the amount of hating he was witnessing. Rachel looked equally surprised. Rachel didn't know either of us that well, but she knew enough about family to know that what I was saying was inappropriate – even if it was true.

After sizing up the hater standing before them, Todd and Rachel looked at each other. I stared back at both of them. Feeling like I'd just shut their love connection down, I moved towards Rachel and was about to gently escort her back into the party.

"C'mon on Boss Lady, it's time to go cut your birthday cake," I said as I grabbed Rachel's hand.

Rachel looked at me and then glanced at Todd. Suddenly from out of nowhere, Rachel and Todd burst into laughter. They even embraced as they laughed.

"Child please! I'm a grown-ass woman!" Rachel said acerbically.

"Yes you are!" Todd said with a devilish grin as he looked down at Rachel's plump butt. He was already envisioning what he was going to do to the birthday girl if he got a chance.

Todd and Rachel started to walk towards the showroom and totally ignored me. I was seething. I grabbed my brother's elbow and asked him to stay a moment longer and talk to me.

"Rachel, could you give my brother and me a moment alone? I need to talk to him."

Rachel looked back and winked at Todd. "Todd, don't leave without getting' with me first. I'm going to hold you to that dinner offer. While y'all talk I'm gonna run to the restroom."

As soon as Rachel opened the showroom door, I lit into my brother.

"What are you doing?" I barked.

"What do you mean?" asked Todd, clearly confused by my attitude.

"You know what the hell I mean! Why would you come here and flirt with my boss? You know I just got this job. If you start dating her and the shit doesn't work out between the two of you, she's gonna take it out on me!"

"So that's why you came out here hatin' on me. You scared I'ma get your boss sprung. Damn Kim, I knew you used to be a hater when we were kids, but I thought you had grown out of that."

"And I knew you were a horny little idiot when we were kids, but I see you haven't grown out of that."

"So, it's like that? You're gonna come out here and blast me like this simply because I'm kickin' it with your boss. You sound like a little scared office flunky," said Todd, and then he started mocking me and talking like the old black people that played butlers and mammies in those 1920's and 1930's films: *Don't mess this up for me Todd. The massa beenz good to us. Iza ain't skilled enuf to move up the corporate ladder on my own so Iza wanna keep my boss happy so Iza can gets me a raise and live like the other buppies. Iza just a few raises away from buying me an overpriced Jaguar Iza can't really afford; so uza betta not mess this up for me.*

"Whatever Todd! You can go back to slingin' those beers at that bar, and take your ghetto-ass friends with you. Better yet, you should take yo ass back to Alabama or New Orleans. Honestly, I don't care where you go, just stay away from me."

15

Todd

Kim walked away leaving me wondering what had happened. I purposely stood outside for another ten minutes as I reflected on the night's events and tried to recall if I'd done anything wrong. Did I say something offensive to her? Was I acting loud and boisterous while inside the party? Or was she simply angry because I'd reappeared in her life?

As much as I wanted to attribute Kim's negative disposition to the stress of her new job, deep down inside I knew that her issues with me had little to do with Rachel, and a lot to do with our past.

I walked back into the party determined to find my rowdy friends. I was going to get Bubba out of that party before he flirted with some man's wife and started a fight; Shakey before he got stinking drunk; and Compulsive before he could tell someone a lie like—he was an illegitimate son of President Obama.

During my time of reflection, I had also decided that I would try to reach out to my sister and squash our beef. I knew it was going to be tough considering all of our negative emotional baggage, but I was going to try anyway.

I knew that reconciliation with Kim was going to be further complicated by the fact that I had no intentions of breaking off contact with Rachel. Rachel had the look, attitude, and status that made her seem unapproachable to most men. But I wasn't like most men. What I lacked in resources, I more than made up for in charisma. The moment I met Rachel I instantly viewed her as a challenge; the type that a man with an ego the size of mine simply had to conquer.

That next week my posse and I were on the court engaging in another one of our ghetto-style basketball games.

"Foul!" shouted Bubba.

"Foul? Your big ass is always callin' a foul!" replied Shakey as he angrily snatched the ball from Bubba's massive hands.

"Just respect my call. That's all I'm sayin'—you need to respect my call," Bubba shouted.

"That's right, y'all need to respect my partners call," I said in defense of Bubba.

"I ain't gotta respect shit!" barked Shakey. "This nigga weighs over 300 pounds and he cries *foul* if you look at him too hard."

"Don't touch me and I won't have to call a foul," Bubba replied and snatched the ball back.

"I'll bet if we touch your big ass with a donut you wouldn't be cryin' foul," said Compulsive.

"Man I quit. My side hurts," I said.

"I quit too," said Compulsive as he and I walked off the court and sat in our usual spot under the tree.

"Man, y'all brothas act like y'all about 50 years old. This is the second time this month y'all dun quit in the middle of a game," said Bubba.

"Fool we're tired. That was the third game in an hour," Shakey shouted. "Your big ass ain't tired because all you do is stand under the basket and tell Todd to throw the ball to you. The moment somebody comes within five feet of you, you start screamin' *foul* like a lil' punk!"

Bubba grabbed Shakey by the back of his neck and then put him in a headlock.

"Let me go!" Shakey shouted. His voice was muffled because his mouth was pressed up against Bubba's arm pit.

"Apologize," Bubba demanded as he pressed his forearm against Shakey, causing the slender man to fall to his knees.

"Apologize for what?" asked Shakey.

"Apologize for not respecting my call."

"Todd, get him off me," Shakey pleaded.

Neither Compulsive or I could help Shakey because we were too busy laughing hysterically.

"You're on your own, Dog," I said.

"Bubba, please let me go."

"Apologize!"

Shakey struggled to remain conscious, "Bubba, you got my head pressed against your arm pits."

"I know. It's called a head lock, Fool!"

"Well do you know that you're funkier than a New York sewer?"

Shakey's wise crack caused Compulsive and me to laugh even harder. Bubba looked at our response to Shakey's joke and started squeezing harder.

"Apologize for that too," Bubba commanded.

"What?"

"Now you gotta apologize for making fun of Big Bubba's hygiene."

"I'm sorry, Bubba. I'm sorry for not respecting your call and I'm sorry for telling everybody that you're funky."

Bubba finally released his grasp of Shakey. Shakey fell to the ground. He wore a low fade styled hair cut; therefore, his hair wasn't messed up, but he did have a different look that caused us to laugh harder.

"Why y'all laughin'?" Shakey asked.

I regained my composure long enough to point at Shakey's head. "Your whole head is white. Big Bubba's deodorant is smeared all across your hair and forehead."

"Nah, Dog. That's just grease and sweat mixed," replied Shakey.

"Shiiit, that's deodorant," said Compulsive.

"That can't be deodorant," replied Shakey with a chuckle. "You can't be as funky as Bubba is, and have on deodorant."

"You didn't wear your Right Guard, Bubba?" I asked.

"Dog, you know Big Bubba's hygiene game is up to par," Bubba replied as he sniffed under his own arms.

"Whatever, Nigga," said Shakey. "If your big ass was wearing Right Guard that shit must have run Left."

The four of us got the rest of our laughs out, and then sat quietly for a few minutes so we could control our breathing. It was a little after twelve o'clock and the sun was shining, but there was a light steady breeze that made the trees sway and the weather feel perfect.

"So what are y'all getting into tonight?" asked Shakey.

"I'm chillin' tonight," said Bubba. "I'm off til Wednesday night. I gotta go to the club for Ladies Night on Wednesday—they are expecting a big crowd since they remodeled the place."

"Me too," I said. "What you got goin' on Cee?"

"Nothin' much. I'm s'posed to be hookin' up with this little honey I met the other night at that party," Compulsive replied.

"Speakin' of that party, wuz up with you and the birthday girl?" Bubba asked Todd.

"You mean that big fine Amazon chick he was dancin' with?" shouted Shakey.

"Ain't nothin happenin'... yet. We talked on the phone a few times since that night. We're gonna go over to the Cheese Cake Factory and grab a bite to eat."

"That's a good choice," said Bubba. "That's where Big Bubba takes all his dime pieces on the first date. The Cheesecake Factory has decent prices, and a large menu to choose from. Baby Girl can order anything—from seafood to steak to Italian food."

"Your big ass *would* start quoting the menu," said Shakey. "If Bubba don't remember anything about the date, he will definitely remember the menu."

I chuckled. "Man to be honest with you, I'm kinda nervous about meeting up with ole' girl."

"I knew your ass was soft," shouted Compulsive.

"Seriously, Dog. I am a little nervous. This is a six figure chick. I don't know what we have in common. The only thing I can really do for her is break her off some of this *Act Right,"* I said and proudly clutched my crotch.

"What do you call yo shit?" asked Shakey with a chuckle.

"I call it that Act Right; even if a chick has a problem with me, one shot of this, and her ass is gonna start acting right... ya heard me!"

"I likes, I likes," said Compulsive. "You mind if I use that in my routine?"

"You mind if I beat yo' ass?" I replied.

"Look here, Dog," Bubba interjected. "If you need help on your date, Big Bubba can come with you. I'll sit a few tables away and send you signs so you will know what to say."

"Thanks, Dog, but I got this."

"Hold up, Dog. Isn't she your sista's boss?" asked Compulsive.

"Yeah, so what's your point?"

"My point is—you're gonna fuck it up for your sister."

"Man, shut up!" I said.

"I'm serious. You know how women are; they can't separate business from personal. We can fuck a chick and then work with her the next day like nothin' happened—women can't do that."

"That is true," echoed Bubba.

"Man, y'all know that if you sleep with a chick at your job, and then walk past her the next day like nothin' happened, she's gonna get pissed off. That woman will spend the entire day tryin' to catch your ass at the water cooler or somethin', just so that she can ask you what's wrong," said Compulsive.

"That's true, but you're forgettin' one thing," I replied confidently.

"What's that?" asked Compulsive.

"You're forgettin' that I don't work with her," I said, and gave Shakey high five.

"Tee, you too smart to be so damn ignant," Compulsive replied. "As long as I've known you, you don't hang out with one woman for more than two months."

"That's true dog," Bubba blurted out.

Compulsive continued, "The minute you tap that ass and the thrill of the chase is gone, you're gonna kick that woman to the curb. She's gonna be walkin' around with a wet ass and pissed off. Since she won't be able to do anything to you, she's gonna take her anger out on your sister."

"The nigga is a compulsive liar, but he's got a point," said Bubba as he looked at me and then back at Compulsive.

Compulsive showed Bubba his middle finger and then continued, "I'm tellin' you, Dog. Your sista is gonna end up gettin' the short end of the stick if you screw her boss."

I sat with my back against the tree and allowed Compulsive's comments to sink in. I knew in my heart that I'd been guilty of being a womanizer. I knew that I had a fear of commitment. In my private moments, I reasoned that my fears may have been rooted in the possibility that I would develop some of the same disturbing and violent habits as my father.

The only way I knew to avoid misusing a woman while in a relationship was to avoid committing to the relationship in the first place. I had convinced myself that I was actually doing women a favor by loving them and leaving them. This may have been considered warped logic if my theory was ever displayed for the publics opinion, but it wasn't. These were my private thoughts; therefore, only my interpretation of my actions mattered.

The four of us grabbed our bags and left the court. I had a lot to think about. Despite the protest of my buddies, I decided to meet Rachel anyway; a decision that would change my life forever.

16

Rachel

My party was off the chain! I haven't had that much fun in a long time. The turnout was better than I expected. The vibe was perfect, and to top it all off, I made a connection with Todd.

Todd's a little younger than I am—if you consider fourteen years a *little* younger. That doesn't bother me any. As a matter of fact, I consider it to be a compliment. At least I know that all the time I spent at the gym wasn't wasted.

Todd seems to be a very interesting guy. I'm going to have dinner with him on Tuesday; I'll be able to gauge his conversation better in a more intimate environment. The only thing that was weird about my party was Kim's behavior. It was clear to me—and anyone paying attention—that she wasn't too happy with her brother and I becoming friendly. If she has any sense she'd sit back and let nature take its course. She could end up reaping a lot of the rewards.

I spent the next day after my party recuperating. Cupcake was sleeping at a friend's house for the entire weekend so I had a lot of time to focus on me and some of my pending issues.

After lying in bed until noon on Saturday, I finally got up, showered and headed to my meeting with the person who was now my biggest nuisance. We met at a coffee shop downtown. The place was crowded and noisy—I felt like a low budget spy passing off classified documents to the enemy.

I arrived fifteen minutes early just to check the place. Much to my surprise, the person I was coming to meet was already there waiting for me.

"I didn't think you were going to show up."

"Whatever… let's just get this over with," I replied.

I pulled an envelope containing ten thousand dollars in cash—half of the bonus money I received earlier in the year. I didn't want to part with my money, but I needed this clown to go away and leave me alone.

"Aren't you going to count it?"

"I will, but not here in public. Besides, I don't believe you will do anything stupid like bring less money than you said."

"Well, do you have what you were supposed to bring?"

"Yes I do. Here it is."

"Is this the only copy?" I asked.

"Yep."

"How do I know you didn't make other copies?"

"You don't. You're just gonna have to trust me."

"Yeah right. I wouldn't trust you if my life depended on it."

"That's not true because right now your life does depend on this. You have to trust me whether you want to or not."

I examined the paperwork. Everything appeared to be in order. This document could ruin me. I'd worked so hard to escape my past and Lecar, this was the last remaining thing that could turn my world upside down. Now that I had this in my possession, all I had to do was allow my attorney to address the task of getting rid of Lecar and all the remaining negativity associated with him.

Without saying another word, I stood up and walked away. I never looked back. That was one person's face I never wanted to see again.

17

Kim

That next Monday at work, the office seemed unusually quiet. Many of the assistants stayed glued to their desks. The Executives, including Rachel, all had their office doors closed. That was the universal sign to everyone that unless it was an urgent matter, don't bother them.

It was the type of quiet that usually followed an office party. Most people get so drunk that they forget what they've done to embarrass themselves or someone else. The cure for this awkward aftermath is usually two or three days of segregation—that's usually how long it takes before the office gossip starts to subside.

While most people sat around hoping that their name wasn't being bantered around, Lucas stood tall inside of his little kingdom smirking at the people whom he already had the dirt on.

It didn't take long for me to learn the gossip patterns of my new workplace. After ensuring that Rachel had everything she needed for her first meeting that morning, I strolled down to Lucas' area—the place where rumors were born and died.

"Hey Lucas," I said nervously.

"What's up, Kim?"

"Nothin'—I'm just strecthin' my legs. I didn't see you this morning when I came in. I didn't think you were here today."

"Yeah, I've been here—dealin' with some of these needy folks. By nine o'clock, I'd already let three highly educated employees inside their offices; changed one woman's flat tire; and escorted a half dozen vendors to the secured areas up there where you work. I was probably doing some of that stuff when you passed by."

Lucas paused for a moment and then smiled at me. "So, are you fully recuperated from that party you threw for your boss last Friday night?"

"I didn't throw anything for her, she threw herself a party. I was just the party planner."

"Well, from what I've heard, you did a heck of a job."

I was relieved to hear that. I was having a difficult time gauging whether or not people felt the party was a success.

"Is that all you heard?"

"What do you mean?"

"Lucas, don't play with me. I know that if there is anyone in this building who knows about anything scandalous that took place at that party, it's you."

The slight grin on Lucas' face was all I needed to see to know that there was something being whispered that I needed to know about.

"Give it up," I insisted.

"Give what up?" Lucas asked coyly.

"Don't play with me. Give up the dirt. I can tell you are dying to tell me something."

"I didn't hear much… other than your boss seemed to have a good time."

"I'm listening."

"Well, rumor has it that your boss was on the dance floor getting felt up by a dude wearing dreadlocks."

It took everything within me to keep from screaming out loud. After spending a few seconds imploding, I found the courage to ask Lucas to elaborate.

"Tell me what you know. Am I gonna have to do some damage control around here?"

"Nawh, I don't think it's that serious. From what I hear, a few of the executives were there getting their drink on. I'm sure her little scene wasn't the worst. As a matter of fact, I heard two women were seen in the female bathroom kissing, a woman was seen in the men's bathroom, and one person vomited inside one of those fancy cars."

"You're lying?"

"Nope… that's what I heard. That's why I don't think anyone's going to remember seeing Rachel getting felt up on the dance floor. Besides, she was the birthday girl. The host of the party always gets a pass.

"Although I must admit, I didn't think Rachel was the type of woman that would mess with a guy wearing dreadlocks. She comes across as way too stiff and uptight for that. But, you know what happens when people get that liquor in their system—their true personality comes out."

I was about to respond, but before I could, Lucas and I got the shock of our lives.

Rachel emerged from the hallway. She looked at me and then at Lucas and asked, "So Lucas, what else did you hear about me that I should be aware of?"

Lucas looked like he wanted to shit on himself right there. I'm sure he could feel his nuts shriveling as he searched for a response. When a good comeback eluded him, he shuffled a stack of papers and stuttered, "Oh, uhh, hey Mrs.—I mean Ms. Biko."

"Oh, I'm Ms. Biko now," Rachel replied in a stern tone. "C'mon Lucas, tell me some of things you heard that people were saying about me."

Lucas looked as helpless as a defendant being scolded by Judge Mathis on that courtroom television show. Sensing that my new office buddy was close to expelling all of his bodily fluids, I decided to intervene. The decision to bail him out wasn't that hard, I owed Lucas for covering for me when I was late for work on my first day. This was an opportune time for me to return the favor.

"Excuse us for a second, Lucas," I said as I gently grabbed Rachel by the elbow and led her into the hallway. "I think you may have misinterpreted what just happened. Lucas called me down here to inform me of the office gossip that was spreading about your party.

"He and I were just sitting here scheming on how we were going to keep your name out of it. We both understand the importance of your roll here at this company. Every black person here has a vested interest in you succeeding. Hell, every since my first day on the job, Lucas has been the main person preaching to me about how I need to make sure you are protected because there are people here who would love to see you fail."

"Oh really," Rachel replied, in a negative tone.

"Rachel, Lucas is probably your biggest fan. Besides, I know for a fact he wouldn't talk bad about you."

"And how do you know that?" asked Rachel, as she stood there with her arms crossed wearing a scowl on her face.

"I know that because I believe he has a crush on you. That man would drink your bath water."

I considered myself to be rather savvy when it came to office politics. Cleaning this up would require all of my diplomacy skills. I learned early in life that the best way to calm down an angry narcissist was to stroke his or her ego—so I started stroking.

Rachel looked me up and down, and then glanced over at Lucas. The poor man was so nervous, he was guzzling a bottle of water and dabbing a folded napkin on his forehead at the same time. I could tell that Rachel was still trying to figure me out. Until she became more familiar with me, Rachel would have to take my word as the gospel.

She looked over at Lucas one last time and rolled her eyes at him. "Look, the reason I came looking for you is because my 11:30 a.m. meeting has been canceled. I'm taking an early lunch—would you like to join me?"

"Uhh, yeah. I would love to," I replied as I tried to mask my excitement. I'd only been working for a few weeks and Rachel was already inviting me to lunch for the second time.

"Let me run upstairs and grab my purse. I'll be right back."

18

Rachel

While Kim went upstairs to grab her purse, I sauntered over to Lucas' desk. I didn't trust him, and I wanted him to know it.

"So, now you are one of my biggest fans around here? You got that girl fooled already."

Lucas looked like a whipped puppy. He glanced up at me and then looked at his computer screen.

"I thought we had an understanding. You really are pushing me. You may think I'm gullible, but don't get it twisted; you don't want to get on my bad side."

I wanted to reach across that desk and punch him in the mouth. Lucas was a phony; it just blew me away that no one else could see it. I know that he was silently calling me all types of bitches and whores inside of his head as I walked away, but he didn't dare say that stuff out loud.

When Kim returned we went to a nearby restaurant. The scene was a little awkward at first, but I decided to get the conversation started by asking her some very blunt questions.

"So Kim, can I ask you something?"

"Sure, go ahead."

"Why were you bothered the other night when you saw me talking to your brother?"

Kim nearly choked. She wasn't expecting that question. She swallowed her food and then took a gulp of her drink to wash it down. The entire time she tried to digest her food I sensed that her mind was racing for a good answer.

"Before you answer let me say this," I said. "I like people to be straight up with me. One of the things I like about you is that you don't act intimidated when you are around me. Even if you are intimidated you hide it well. I can't stand being around weak people. So, with that being said, I need you to stop searching for the *politically correct* answer, and tell me your true feelings."

Kim smiled at me. It was as if she'd been waiting for the green light so that she could open up and be candid.

"Okay Rachel, I'm gonna keep it real with you. When I saw you and Todd at that party I could see the sparks flying instantly. A few moments later, when I saw the two of you bumping and grinding…"

"Bumping and grinding?" I asked, surprised at the way she characterized our dancing.

"Yes, bumping and grinding," replied Kim sheepishly.

"Go ahead, finish your thought."

"Well, when I saw you and Todd dancing, I got nervous."

"Why?"

"Because, I really want to keep this job."

"What does my decision to dance with Todd have to do with you working for me?"

"It has a lot to do with him if you are going to date him. If the two of you don't work out then it's going to be awkward for me. If he makes you mad—which I know my brother is capable of doing—I was concerned that you would take your anger out on me. I figured that you might fire me because of something he does."

"I wouldn't do that," I replied.

"Do you intend to see him?" Kim asked.

"Yes I do. Do you have a problem with that?"

"Does it matter what I think?" asked Kim.

"No. I just wanted to know your thoughts," I replied without looking up from my plate.

"Well, since I answered your question I feel it's only fair that you answer one of mine?"

I gently patted my top lip and the corners of my mouth with my napkin. I took a sip of my drink and then sat back in my seat.

"Go ahead. Ask your question."

Kim hesitated for a second. She wasn't sure if she should ask the question she wanted answered the most. She definitely had several other areas she could have asked some cogent questions about: mentoring opportunities, the company's management program, etc. But, Kim was a risk taker, and much like me, she said what she meant and meant everything she said.

"You say that you are going to see him again."

"That's right."

"Well that's fine and dandy, but are you gonna tell him about the tension between you and your ex-husband?"

"Excuse me?" I asked. The mere mention of my ex-husband caused me to raise my voice.

I guess Kim sensed that she'd ventured down the wrong road so she immediately tried to clean up her question.

"I'm just asking because I am a little concerned. After all, Todd and I don't have the best relationship, but he is still my little brother. I don't want him stepping into any drama. I don't want him to be attacked by some out of control ex-husband, and end up on the news.

"Rachel, I just heard you on the phone talking about your ex-husband. Forgive me if I'm out of line, but it doesn't sound like the two of you have the best relationship. I'm just looking out for Todd."

I was annoyed by Kim's line of questioning, but understood her concern. I took another sip of my drink as I formulated my retort.

"Kim, I don't usually talk about my personal life, but I do believe you make a good point. I don't have any siblings, but if I had a sibling I would ask the same question.

"My ex-husband and I had a very hostile divorce. He is from Johannesburg, South Africa and has some very strong views about African-Americans. He also believes that women should be submissive. I'm sure you can tell from the short time that you've worked for me that I'm not the woman whose going to put up with that type of attitude."

"No. I could never see you accepting that from a man."

"I moved here to Atlanta from San Francisco where he and I lived. I got full custody in the divorce and he is still pissed off. I had to get a restraining order because he has tried twice to take my daughter. He wants to bring her back to Africa. If he takes her I know that I will never see her again.

"The man you heard me shouting at on the phone is my attorney, Lance. He is supposed to be taking care of some pending financial issues. I pay Lance a lot for his services, and I don't believe he's been earning it. I shouted at him to let him know that I'm not going to let him beat me out of my money. I stay on his back to make sure he handles my business."

"I'm sorry to hear that you are dealing with all that drama," said Kim compassionately.

"I appreciate that, but I'm going to be fine. Now back to your brother; Todd and I hit it off well. We spoke two or three times this weekend and have agreed to meet each other for dinner and drinks tomorrow night."

"Damn, y'all don't waste time," said Kim.

"I promise you, I won't hurt Todd. Besides, based on what I saw, he can handle himself."

19

Kim

Rachel's last comment was a little more than what I wanted to hear. I don't care to visualize anything sexual involving my brother. I frowned openly, put my hand over my mouth, and pretended I was about to puke. Rachel burst into laughter, and we continued to enjoy our meal.

The more I spoke to Rachel, the more I liked her. She was tough and standoffish because she had to be, not because she enjoyed being difficult. That's the only way a woman can make it and subsequently survive in Corporate America. Rachel and I were a lot alike. I was absolutely convinced that she would make a great mentor.

As we drove back to the office I decided to exploit the current synergy and ask Rachel a few questions about her daughter.

"So how is your daughter?"

"Oh she's fine. She can be a handful at times, but for the most part she's a sweet child."

"How has she dealt with not being able to see her dad regularly?"

"She's adjusting. If she hasn't adjusted, she will eventually."

I was a little surprised by Rachel's answer. She didn't express one drop of sympathy for the child's feelings. She may have been a mover and shaker in the corporate world, but I could tell she wasn't the most maternal woman walking around. She definitely wasn't anything like my mother. There was something in her tone that suggested she didn't really want to discuss Cupcake, so I didn't pursue the topic any further. I was making strides with this woman so, I wasn't about to let my curiosity disrupt my progress.

Tuesday was by far the most stressful work day I'd experienced while working at Boxxmore. Several members of the Board of Directors were visiting, and it caused many of the executives to act like idiots. Tensions were high. I couldn't wait for quitting time.

The traffic on I-75 was very bad. Moving at a snail's pace, I was trapped in the middle lane with no option other than to deal with the log jam. To make matters worse, the gas tank light on my dashboard started to chime and blink. That was all the motivation I needed to start bullying the drivers to the right of me so that I could exit.

After finding a gas station and putting my last nine dollars in my tank, I continued my trek home. Visions of soaking in a nice hot bubble bath were interrupted by my cell phone.

"Hello."

"Kim?" asked the unfamiliar voice.

"Yes, this is Kim."

"Hey, this is Rachel."

Surprise doesn't begin to describe my reaction. I immediately started to wonder if there was something I'd forgotten to do at the office before I left.

"Hey Boss Lady. Is everything okay?"

"Yes and no. You did an awesome job at work today. That PowerPoint presentation you whipped up for me was well received by the Board Members."

"I'm glad to hear that," I replied, and then thrust my fist in the air in celebration. "If the presentation went well, what's the problem?"

"I know this is short notice, but I need your help."

Fine by me; this is just another chance for me to rack up brownie points.

"No problem. What do you need?"

"I need a babysitter."

"Excuse me?"

"A babysitter. I need a sitter. The girl I normally use is unavailable. I'm supposed to meet Todd for dinner tonight. I don't want to cancel our plans so I decided to call you. I figured you would understand. After all, you did lecture me the other day about how much you want to look out for him. I know you wouldn't want him to be stood up on a date."

Damn, this bitch is bold. The very tenacious attitude I admire is now being used against me. I had plans to take a bath, drink some wine, and fall asleep while reading a book. Watching some snot nose kid was not on my agenda. She must be crazy if she thinks she can just call me at the last minute and expect me to jump through a hoop like this.

"Of course I'll watch her," I replied. "I didn't have any plans."

"Great. I'm going to email the directions to my house to you. If you could come over at around 6:30 p.m. that would be perfect."

"That's no problem," I replied. Before I could say anything else Rachel had hung up the phone.

This is some bullshit! She's lucky I wasn't that into the book I was reading.

My first thought when I walked into Rachel's house was, *this woman needs an interior decorator.* The walls were bare. The rooms were spacious, but lacked vibrancy. The furniture looked expensive, but there wasn't a theme or any flow to anything. Much like her clothing, Rachel's house appeared to be owned by someone with a lot of money, but very little style.

Rachel escorted me and appeared to be a little flustered. She was acting like a person who'd never been on a date before. While she gave me a few last minute details about Cupcake, my eyes searched the bottom level of the house for a glimpse of the child.

"I'm telling you now Kim, Cupcake can be manipulative. She will probably wait until I leave and then hit you with a sad face, and then ask you to give her some cookies. Don't fall for it! Her butt is too chubby already—I'm trying to wean her off of sweets."

I nodded my head to signal I understood, but the entire time she talked I thought she sounded overly critical of the kid. She's an eight year old child—asking for a cookie is what they do.

"So where is Cupcake?" I asked.

Rachel stopped dead in her tracks, turned around slowly, and looked at me.

"Please refer to her as Danielle."

Damn, is it that serious? She acts like the child is in hiding or something - like she's in the witness protection program. Referring to her as Cupcake isn't a crime.

"My apologies. I've heard you refer to her by her nickname so often that I thought it was okay."

Before Rachel could answer, Cupcake came walking down the stairs.

"Mommy, are you about to leave?"

"Yes I am. This is Ms. Kim; she's going to watch you for a few hours until I return. I expect you to listen to her and be a good girl. I won't be gone too long."

"Yes, Ma'am," Cupcake replied.

Oh hell no! A few hours are too long. I guess she's just assuming I don't have a life. I know one thing—if she isn't back in two hours I'm going to start blowing up her cell phone.

"Girl, take your time and have fun. Cup… I mean, Danielle and me are going to have a good time. I already told you that I didn't have any plans."

Rachel grabbed her keys, gave Cupcake a hug, and rushed out of the house. Cupcake and I stood there for a few seconds staring at each other. She was sizing me up, and I was doing the same to her. We looked like two kids on the playground trying to determine if the other was worth playing with.

She looked at my hair and then my feet. I was wearing a multi-colored scarf to combat the unseasonably chilly weather. I think she liked it.

"Can I see your scarf?"

"Yes, you can."

Cupcake stared at the scarf and allowed her little hand to glide across it. "It's pretty. Can I have it?"

"You can't have it, but you can wear it for a little while."

"Really!"

"Yes. It's yours for the time I'm here tonight," I replied. The ice was officially broken.

I peeked out the window to make sure Rachel was gone, and then I toured the house. I was eager to see how a six-figure sista lived. The décor was nothing like I expected.

Lucas described Rachel as devout Christian; therefore, I was expecting to see paintings and artifacts that reflected her religious beliefs, but none were present. There were no pictures of Jesus Christ hanging on the cross. No crosses on dressers or mounted over door frames. In fact, there was nothing in Rachel's house that signified she was some type of bible toting Christian. Her walls were adorned with eclectic pieces of art. Her furniture was contemporary and stylish. I was definitely impressed.

"So Danielle, what do you want to do?"

She seemed a little apprehensive at first, but within minutes her bubbly personality started to show. I tried for as long as I could to not enjoy myself, but Cupcake's attitude was infectious. Thirty minutes later she'd completely won me over.

As we sat on the floor in the middle of the living room coloring in two separate coloring books, I could no longer resist the temptation to ask Cupcake a few questions about her mother.

"So Danielle, why does your mom call you Cupcake?"

"Because, that's my favorite food in the whole wide world. Do you like cupcakes?"

"Yes, I do."

"I sure wish I had a cupcake right now."

I'll bet you do, but it will be a cold day in hell before I ever give you one.

"So tell me Danielle, do you like your house?"

"Yes, but I like my old house better."

"What do you like about your old house?"

"I had a lot of friends to play with. We had a park next to our house and I used to go out and play with my friends."

As Cupcake sat there coloring, I noticed something strange on her knees. It looked like little black pin marks. Upon closer examination I realized that they were scabs.

"What happened to your knees?" I asked.

Cupcake stopped coloring long enough to rub her hand over her knee and reply, "That's the marks from the rice."

"The rice? What do you mean?"

The child put her head down and started coloring again. A few second she pointed towards the kitchen and said, "The rice from the refrigerator. Mommy had to punish me because I was being bad. She makes me put my knees on the rice."

"She makes you kneel on the rice when she wants to punish you?"

Cupcake didn't reply verbally. She didn't even look up at me. She just kept coloring and nodded her head.

I'll be damned. She's not only mean at the office, Rachel's like that woman in the movie, "Mommie Dearest". I'll bet this child can't have any wire hangers in her closet either.

I could tell that this child would answer any question I asked, so I took advantage of it. I contemplated my next one. I knew by asking it I would probably be crossing the line, but I was itching to know.

"So Danielle, tell me about your daddy. Do you miss him?"

Cupcake stopped coloring. She looked at me and then put her head down and started coloring again.

"Umm, I don't have a daddy. My mommy is my daddy."

The child's answer surprised me initially, but the more I thought about it the more understandable it seemed. Growing up in the 'hood, I'd been around enough single parent households to know that frustrated mother's often told their kids that they were mommy and daddy because a lot of times they were performing both roles. Based on what I'd observed and heard up to that point, Rachel definitely fell in that category.

Even though it may have been accurate that Rachel was forced to act as mommy and daddy, I still found it disturbing that she would plant that seed in the child's head. There are just some things kids shouldn't be exposed too. Although my father abandoned me, I never heard my mother say anything negative about him. But, not everyone conducted themselves with the level of class and dignity as my mother.

20

Todd

The restaurant was relatively empty on a Tuesday night. The staff outnumbered the customers. Every clank of the plates and spoons could be heard in the dining room area. The shouts from the cooks back in the kitchen could be heard all the way in the front near the entrance.

Rachel and I were scheduled to meet at seven o'clock that evening. She was there ten minutes early. I on the other hand, was ten minutes late. I did call to let Rachel know I would be running a few minutes late, but that didn't seem to win me any brownie points with her.

"Hey, Boo. I'm sorry I'm late," I said as I sat down.

"You are ten minutes late," Rachel replied as she glanced at her watch and then up at me. "I was gonna give you five more minutes and then leave."

"Boo, I called you in advance."

"First of all, you callin' in advance doesn't change the fact that it's not a good look to be ten minutes late for a first date. Secondly, I'm not your boo. You don't even know me like that."

Damn this chick has got a whole lot of attitude. I should have known she was the uptight type. I can tell already that this ain't gonna work out.

"You know Rachel, you are right. I should have made a better effort to get here on time. We never get a second chance to make a first impression, and I guess I messed up my shot. As far as the *boo* thing, that's a bad habit of mine. Please accept my apology."

"Look Todd, I think it's important that you know some things about me. I am always on time; therefore, I expect the people I deal with—whether business or personal—to be on time. I can't stand CP time. That's what's wrong with black folk now; we've accepted tardiness like it's cool. There is nothing cool or cute about being late. That's just perpetuating the stereotype.

"As far as the *boo* thing, I just felt compelled to let you know about that. I wasn't trying to act stuck up or anything, but my name ain't boo—and you know that. Let's learn a little bit about each other before we start calling each other nicknames. These are my standards, if they are too much for you to handle just let me know."

I felt like I'd been punched in the gut. I was both offended and impressed at the same time. On one hand I thought that Rachel was making an innocent mistake into a federal case. On the other hand, I wasn't accustomed to being blasted like that. I'd been in Rachel's presence for less than five minutes and could already tell that she was the most confidant woman I'd ever dealt with. It was refreshing to me and to a certain degree—a turn on.

Despite the bumpy start, the rest of our dinner date went on without a hitch. Rachel told me about her daughter, Danielle and her job. She avoided talking about her ex-husband Lecar.

I told Rachel about my life as a bartender; my desire to be a famous author; and how I ended up in Atlanta. I avoided talking about my severely damaged relationship with my sister Kim.

As much as I was impressed with Rachel's bluntness, I did notice that she seemed a little aggressive. She stared down the waiter if he took a minute or two too long to tend to our table. She sent her plate back twice because her salmon was not cooked perfectly. She even snatched the bill before I could grab it. I was impressed with her eagerness to pay the bill, but I was somewhat annoyed by her scrutiny of the $42 bill.

Damn Rachel, you make six figures and drive a damn Jaguar, why are you breakin' down a $42 bill?

By the time we were finishing our meals and preparing to leave, the restaurant had become somewhat crowded. When we exited, I held the door open for three very attractive women that were entering.

It didn't go unnoticed by me—or Rachel—that one of the women took a double glance in my direction. I surprised myself when I gave a casual smile and looked away. In the past I would have used my eyes to send all types of subliminal messages to the woman. But, I didn't this time. I'd already botched the beginning of our date, now that I'd rebounded successfully, I didn't want to say or do anything to mess things up.

I walked Rachel to her car and stood next to the door as she opened it. I was expecting a friendly hug and maybe a quick kiss on the cheek, but all I got was a lame *thank you,* and a head nod.

"Damn, that's all I get?"

"That's all you deserve," she replied. "If you want more than that I would suggest you go and get a kiss and hug from one of those women you held the door open for and was grinning at."

"Rachel, I was just being polite."

"You were flirting!" Rachel barked. "You don't think I saw you smiling at that first one?"

"Man, yo ass is trippin'," I said in a frustrated tone.

Rachel didn't appreciate my insolent reply. She took her partially opened door and shoved it all the way open—causing it to hit my thighs and kneecaps.

"Ouch! What's your problem woman?"

"I don't have a problem, you have the fuckin' problem," Rachel shouted. "You are so used to dealin' with hoochies that you can easily disrespect; you don't know how to handle a real woman. You've been disrespecting me since this date started. First you were late; then you called me some ghetto-ass nickname—without my permission; and then you stood in my face and *eye fucked* another woman.

"I don't have a problem; you are the one who has *problems*. And don't call me again until you've fixed *your problems*."

Rachel sat in her car, slammed the door, and then pulled out of that parking space like a race car driver pulling out of the pit stop. She was so callous and reckless; her front tire almost ran over my foot.

I stood there looking like a lost child. I rubbed my knees and thighs, and even checked my foot for possible damage. Like a person who'd just stumbled inexplicably while walking, I looked around the parking lot to see if anyone had witnessed what happened.

As I walked back to my car my anger increased to the point that I disregarded my own belief that women shouldn't be called a bitch.

"That bitch is crazy," I mumbled. "Fine as wine, but crazy as hell."

I went straight home and put an ice pack on my knee. It wasn't swelling, but an hour had passed since Rachel struck it with the car door and it was still smarting.

I replayed the events of the evening to try to determine if I was grossly negligent or if Rachel was in need of an enema. I concluded that the answer fell somewhere in between.

"I don't think I violated enough to warrant her reacting that way," I mumbled. "But, I did screw up a few times. She's definitely unlike any woman I've ever dealt with. She's definitely worth the effort. I'm going to see if she'll give me a second chance."

21

Kim

I could hear the garage door open when Rachel returned from her date. Danielle and I were sitting on the sofa in the living room eating popcorn and watching *Finding Nemo.*

"Uhh ohh. That's Mommy!" shouted Danielle nervously. "I'm not supposed to eat popcorn or watch movies on a school night.

Shit, I wish you would've told me that before you went and stuck the movie in the DVD.

As Danielle leaped up the bowl of popcorn spilled all over the sofa and floor. The child stopped dead in her tracks and stared at the popcorn.

"We gotta get this up before Mommy comes inside," said Danielle. The child was in an all out panic.

"Calm down, Baby. I'll clean it up."

Danielle stood there for a few seconds longer and then ran up the stairs.

"Danielle, it's okay, Baby," I yelled as I tried to sweep up the popcorn."

"What's okay?" asked Rachel as she walked in.

"Umm, we had a little accident. Danielle—I mean, I spilled the popcorn on the floor. I'm nearly finished cleaning it up."

"Why is Cupcake eating popcorn on a Tuesday? She knows that I don't allow that!"

I don't know what happened on that date, but it was clear that Rachel returned in a foul mood. She tapped her feet and watched me as I picked up every kernel from off of her sofa. My instincts told me that Danielle was going to be in a ton of trouble the moment I left. I had visions of Rachel making the child stay up all night scrubbing the floor with Comet or some type of detergent. I knew I needed to say something to try to save this child from the tyrant standing over me.

"Rachel, it really was my fault. As a matter of fact, Danielle tried to…"

"Cupcake! Get your butt down here now!"

Rachel's voice was booming. I was frightened to the point that my hand was shaking; so I knew that the child must have been terrified.

I couldn't believe that some popcorn on the floor caused this type of reaction. Rachel seemed a little hot-headed, but this was a little over the top. There must have been something that ticked her off earlier.

Dammit Todd! What did you do?

"Yes, Ma'am," said Danielle, as she kneeled down and looked at Rachel from between the bars on the staircase railing. Her little legs were shaking and her knees were knocking together as the fear of her mother's possible reaction started to set in.

"I said get down here," Rachel reiterated.

Danielle commenced to walking down the stairs. She walked gingerly, like she was afraid there was a land mine under each step. She stopped at the bottom of the staircase. I didn't blame her for not coming near Rachel; I was tempted to run my ass up those steps too.

"Are you supposed to eat popcorn during the week?"

"No, Ma'am."

"Did you tell Ms. Kim you aren't supposed to eat popcorn during the week?"

My heart went out to the child. I wanted to run over and grab Danielle and hug her… until I heard her response.

"Yes, Ma'am. I told Ms. Kim you didn't want me to eat popcorn."

What the… no this little big-head child didn't just stand there and tell a bold face lie.

I wanted to call Danielle a liar so bad my bottom lip started to quiver. I looked at Danielle with a pleading look on my face. I could see the fear in her eyes. I could hear the anguish in her voice. I noticed how her legs twitched. She started rubbing her knee caps together like she had to urinate. I'd experienced it before. Todd's father Kennedy caused me to have several moments like the one Danielle was having.

I empathized with her fear. My eyes were saying to Danielle, *Baby, it's gonna be alright – just tell the truth.*

Danielle was too young to understand the meaning of words like *integrity* or *ethics.* She didn't just respect her mother, she feared her. Unfortunately for me, Danielle's fear superseded my plea for her to do the right thing.

Danielle's innocent little eyes spoke back to me and replied, *Ms. Kim I'm sorry, but my mama's crazy as hell! It's either you or me. It will be a cold day in hell before I ever admit to asking for that popcorn. You're on your own.*

Yep, Danielle left me hanging. I stood there feeling like an idiot. Here I was trying to cover for her, and she threw my ass right under the bus. I didn't look in Rachel's direction, but I could feel her piercing glare.

"I'm gonna finish cleaning this up and then leave," I mumbled and stared down at the floor.

Rachel didn't say another word. She threw her purse on the sofa and then walked into her bedroom.

"Go get ready for bed!" she ordered Danielle and then closed the door.

I cleaned up the remaining kernels and then left. I spent my entire ride home wishing I'd never agreed to baby-sit Danielle's little greedy ass.

I knew that Rachel was not going to be in a good mood that next day at work. Between that popcorn incident and whatever my brother did on that date to piss her off, I was actually expecting to be fired.

I arrived at work thirty minutes early so that I could make sure everything I had to do was taken care of. The only thing I could control was my performance; therefore, I focused on making sure Rachel didn't have any convenient work related excuses to get rid of me.

Reports were completed. Jelly donuts were warmed and ready. A cup of Brazilian blend coffee was sitting on her desk ready to be slurped. I was in total ass-kissing mode, and I'm not ashamed to admit it.

As I sat at my desk trying to remember if there was anything I'd missed, Lucas came through the door.

"Hello, Kim."

"Hey. What brings you up here?"

"I had to escort this gentleman up," Lucas replied, and then gestured to a guy carrying a dozen long stemmed yellow roses.

"For me?"

"I'm afraid not," Lucas replied, trying to muffle his chuckle.

"I have a delivery for Rachel Biko," said the delivery man.

I took the beautiful roses from the delivery man and placed them on Rachel's desk. There was a card sticking out. I swear that card was calling my name. I wondered if it was from Todd. I know it was presumptuous of me to think that, but I'd been working for Rachel for a few weeks and hadn't seen any signs of another man in her life.

I was about to walk out of her office, but I had to read it. I looked over my shoulder to make sure I was alone. When I picked up the card and examined the seal to see if it was loose. Fortunately, it wasn't sealed at all.

I opened the envelope and was about to pull out the card, but from out of nowhere a voice called my name.

"Kim, you wanna explain to me why you are in my office?"

Shit! I'm busted!

22

Rachel

Kim looked like a dear caught in head lights. I couldn't tell what she was fumbling with on my desk, but the look on her face told me she was snooping.

"Oh. Hey, Rachel, I was just placing these beautiful roses on your desk."

When she moved to the side I could see a dozen long stemmed roses. Kim was holding the card that came with them.

"Why do you have the card in your hand?" I asked.

"This card?"

"Yes that card."

"It fell on the floor. I was just about to stick it back inside of the flower package."

I deliberately remained quiet and stared at Kim for a few seconds. I wanted to see if I could spot any facial expressions that would indicate she was lying, but I couldn't.

"Well, thank you. That will be all."

Kim stuck the card in the package and walked past me.

"I'm going to be working on some stuff so don't let any calls through unless they are urgent."

"Okay."

I sat down at my desk and examined the roses. I couldn't deny their beauty. The buds hadn't opened and the stems were long—good quality. The leaves on the stems were a deep green, which indicated they were fresh.

I opened the card and read it.

Rachel,

I obviously offended you yesterday. That wasn't my intent. I'm sorry. I would appreciate it if you gave me a second chance. I will be at the same spot tonight at 7 waiting on you. Please meet me so that we can talk. I hope you show…I will be on time. ☺

Todd

I guess he got my point. I needed to think about accepting his invitation. I've never been big on giving people second chances, but Todd was extremely charming…and fine.

I decided to give him a second chance. If he blew it again, he was gonna get the axe… his sister too.

23

Todd

I was up all night thinking about Rachel. I couldn't put my finger on it, but I was extremely attracted to her. She wasn't the prettiest woman I'd ever dealt with. She wasn't even the shapeliest. But by far, the feistiest woman I'd ever met—I liked that.

I spent my last $60 on a dozen long stem roses. Rachel was so refined and worldly that I had to be smart about the type of flowers I sent. Most women I've dealt with don't even know that there is meaning to different colors. After that disastrous first date, she would have probably thrown a bunch of red roses in the trash. Instead, I chose to send her yellow ones because they represented a new beginning and sincerity. I hoped they would enhance the apology that I attached.

By the time the clock struck eleven o'clock I could no longer wait for her answer. I decided to call her office and hear either an acceptance or rejection straight from the horse's mouth.

Hello. You've reached Rachel Biko's office.

"Kim, is that you?" I asked, surprised to hear my sister's voice. I just assumed that Rachel would answer her own phone.

Todd?

"Yeah, it's me. Wuz up?"

Why are you calling here?

"Damn. Hello to you too," I said indignantly.

Oh… hey. I wasn't expecting to hear your voice.

"I'm trying to reach Rachel. Last night's date didn't end too well."

No shit! She came home pissed off. I figured you dropped the ball.

"Yeah, she got mad at me when she caught some women flirting with me."

You mean she caught you flirting back. Boy, you haven't changed a bit.

"That's where you're wrong. I didn't even flirt back. She just figured I did since one of the chicks was grinning. I didn't do anything. Rachel got a Jekyll and Hyde thing going on."

Yeah she is rather moody. Did you send those flowers?

"Good, the flowers arrived?"

Yeah, they got here a few minutes before she did.

"Well, what was her reaction?"

I don't know. She closed her office door.

"Transfer my call into her office."

I can't do that.

"Why not?"

Because she made it clear when she came in that she didn't want to be disturbed unless it was an emergency. I'm sorry, but your desire to get your mack on doesn't qualify as a big enough emergency for me to risk my job.

Kim's hatin' was starting to get under my skin. My own damn sister was unwilling to help me out. I probably could have gotten more support from a stranger. If I ever wondered whether Kim wished I'd stay away from her world, her deliberate cock blocking squelched any ambiguity I may have had.

As much as I wanted to loose my cool and give Kim a piece of my mine, I knew that attacking her would not help my efforts. Even worse, an argument would only drive an even bigger wedge between Kim and me.

"Well, I'll find out tonight if they worked."

What's happening tonight?

"I invited her to meet me at the same restaurant. Are you gonna babysit her daughter again if she asks?"

Hell no! That little heifer threw me under the bus last night.

"What did she do?"

It's too long to get into right now. All I can tell you is that I'm not babysitting her daughter tonight or any other night for that matter. If she asks I'm going to tell her I have plans.

"Well, wish me luck."

Umm hmm.

"By the way, I still want to meet you for lunch or something so we can sit down and talk."

About what?

"I think we need to talk about the past and our relationship. Things between you and me seem a little strained. I think it's time we clear the air about some things."

Umm hmm.

I hung up the phone feeling hopeful; at least as it pertained to getting a second shot with Rachel. My relationship with Kim was another story. I could sense that she didn't want me around. I think she was holding a grudge from the fight we had. Whatever her beef was with me, I was going to eventually make her spit it out.

In the meantime, I had a standing basketball game to get too. I wasn't sure how well I would be able to perform because my knee was still hurting. My limited mobility would surely put me and Big Bubba's undefeated record at risk. Just as I predicted, Shakey and Compulsive were giving Bubba and me a beat down on the basketball court.

"Ball game!" shouted Compulsive as he sank the winning shot.

"Finally!" yelled Shakey. "I knew we would beat y'all asses today!"

"The only reason y'all won is because Todd couldn't run," said Bubba.

I walked over to our spot and plopped down. With my back against the tree, I took a swig of the bottled water that awaited me.

"Wuz up with your knee?" asked Shakey.

"You wouldn't believe if I told you," I replied while I rubbed it.

"Try me," Shakey replied.

I commenced to telling the three of them about my date with Rachel. I told them every detail—including the incident in the parking lot.

"Damn, Dog. She seems a little hot-headed," said Bubba.

"She's lucky that wasn't me," said Shakey. "I would have put a dent in that damn car. I'll bet she wouldn't try to hit anybody else."

"I feel you, Dog," said Compulsive. "I know you ain't gonna deal with her again."

I didn't reply to his last comment. I took another swig of my drink and looked the other way.

"Dog, are you still thinkin' about seeing that woman again?' asked Bubba.

"Hell yeah, he's gonna see her again. Look at that stupid look on his face. He probably sent her some flowers or something," said Shakey.

I knew I was going to get heckled if I admitted I'd spent my last dollar sending Rachel flowers so I tried to ignore Shakey. But I couldn't hold back my smile.

"You sent her flowers after she damn near made you a paraplegic?" asked Compulsive.

"I sent her a dozen yellow roses," I replied.

All three of them replied simultaneously, "Awwwh!!!"

"You big pussy!" shouted Shakey. "I knew your ass was soft. This bitch damn near chopped off your leg with her door; got you around here hobbling like you got a dick stuck in your booty, and you bought her some flowers! Nigga give me your wallet."

"Why?" I asked.

"I'm about to revoke your playa card," Shakey replied.

"I agree with Shakey," said Bubba.

"You need to be put on probation for about three months," said Compulsive. "After that time, we will re-evaluate your performance to see if it can be re-issued."

I hope you bought her some of those cheap roses they sell at Krogers," said Bubba.

"Nah, I dropped about sixty dollars on the good kind," I replied.

"Awwwh!!" they all shouted again as they raised their hands in the air dismissively.

They all got a good laugh in at my expense, but I didn't care, I felt Rachel was worth it.

"Seriously, Dog. You need to watch her," said Bubba. "She seems like she might have some psycho tendencies."

After witnessing my friend's reaction to the roses, I didn't dare tell them that I'd asked Rachel to meet later that night. They would have skipped *Playa's Probation* and sent me straight into *Playa's Retirement.*

Determined not to make the same mistake twice, I arrived at the restaurant twenty minutes early. Just like the night before, the restaurant had more employees walking around than customers. I commandeered a table and waited patiently for her to arrive.

Seven o'clock came and Rachel hadn't arrived. Ten after— still no Rachel. The waitress came to my table for the third time to ask me if I wanted to order. I believe she was starting to feel sorry for me. I could tell she must have told her co-workers that there was a possibility I'd been stood up because all of the waitresses started glancing my way.

By 7:20 I was about to give up. Just as I was about to call the waiter over and pay for the Diet Coke's I'd demolished, Rachel came walking through the door.

We made eye contact from across the room. Since Rachel and I were the only black people in the restaurant the waitress must have deduced that she was the woman I'd been patiently waiting on. The waitress smiled and gave me the thumbs up sign.

I stood up and greeted Rachel as she approached.

"I didn't think you were going to show up."

"Now you know how it feels," she replied glibly.

"Point taken," I replied, feeling like a child who'd just been reprimanded by his grade school teacher.

We ordered our food and then commenced to eating. Rachel was a little uptight, but was still the most sophisticated woman in the joint. As she ate I couldn't help but stare at her plump lips. I imagined nibbling and sucking on them.

"Are you okay?" she asked, forcing me to temporarily abandon my lustful thoughts.

"Yes I am," I replied. "So tell me, what made you decide to join me this evening?"

"Well, I decided to ignore our first date and give it a second shot," she replied with a smirk. "And the beautiful roses didn't hurt. Thank you."

Finally some feedback on the roses. I took my gas money and bought those things. "I'm glad you liked them."

"They were beautiful."

"Just like you."

"Thank you. So tell me about you."

"What do you want to know?"

"You're an aspiring author right?"

"Yeah."

"Well, when is the first novel going to be released?"

I really didn't know when. I was still struggling to finish it. I hadn't even started searching for a publisher.

"Honestly, I don't know. I'm going to have to find a company to publish the book."

"You haven't started your search yet?"

"No, I haven't."

"What are you waiting on?"

"I have to finish the book first."

"Are you incapable of searching for a publisher while you write? You do know how to multi-task don't you?"

Rachel's question was laced with cynicism. I felt like she was trying to admonish me. I was trying to avoid an argument, but my annoyance with her question must have shown in my response.

"No, I don't know how to multi-task. I'm not smart enough to do two things at once," I replied curtly.

"Don't get an attitude with me," she replied defensively. "I don't know much about the literary industry, but I know that there is an aspiring author on every corner. Everybody's looking for a publisher. If it's like any other career field, the person who hustles the most is the person the catches the breaks."

I couldn't argue with her on that. I'd heard my share of stories about author's who possessed several finished novels, but couldn't get anyone to publish them.

"I feel you on that. I've actually been thinking about self-publishing. I've been saving my nickels."

"How much does it cost?"

"I've heard figures ranging from $3,000 to $6,000."

"I hope you have a lot of nickels," Rachel replied.

Truth be told, I had about $480 in my savings account, and about $100 in my checking account. The entire time we sat there eating I was praying she ate all of her entrée so that she would be too full to even think about ordering dessert.

I was tired of being on the hot seat so I decided to go on the offensive. I was dying to know about her past; especially the chapter regarding her ex-husband.

"I've answered your query. Are you ready to answer a few of my questions?"

"Sure. If I don't like the questions I'll simply decline to respond."

"That's not fair. I've answered all yours."

"You could've chosen not to."

"True that."

"Shoot."

"Okay, I will. Tell me about you. What was your childhood like? Do you have any siblings?"

"I'm an only child."

"Are your parents alive?"

"My parents passed away when I was nineteen. I've been on my own for twenty years. My parents were kind of strict. They didn't let me do much of anything. My mother was very passive and my father… let's just say he had a bad temper.

"I can relate to that. My dad had a mean streak too."

"I doubt if your father was as mean as mine. He used to smack my mother around if the dishes weren't aligned perfectly in the cabinets."

You have no idea what mean *is. Your dad may have been a stickler for uniformity, but I'll bet he didn't murder your mother.*

"I'm sorry to hear that. How did he treat you?"

"Oh he treated me about the same way he treated her. The only difference was that he didn't beat me for messing up the dishes. Nope, his pet-peeve with me was that I acted strange. That was the excuse he used to justify smacking me upside my head and locking me in my bedroom."

"Why did he feel you were strange?"

"Because I spent too much time reading and staying inside. He would have preferred me to put down the books, and get involved with sports—soccer and stuff like that."

I don't know if it was the wine she was drinking that made her loosen up and spill her guts, but she was definitely on a roll. It was the first time she'd let her guard down and acted—well, normal. I liked it.

"My dad was an uneducated man. He dropped out of school at the age of fifteen. Education wasn't his thing. I think he resented the fact that at the age of twelve I could read better than he could.

"My parents died in car crash. When they died I decided that I would change my life. I became determined to start over and do things my own way. I took the money I received from their insurance policies, and put it to good use. I went to college. The rest is history."

So that's why you are so driven and ambitious. You've been trying to prove your father wrong.

"Do you miss the west coast?"

"Nope. I left that life behind me."

"Did you leave your ex in Cali?"

My last question must have caught her off guard because she paused—a fork of shrimp primavera perched an inch from her lips. I know it wasn't the best segue, but I didn't care—I wanted to know.

"Yes. I left Lecar in California," Rachel replied sharply.

"Ouch. Did I strike a nerve?"

"Not really. Your question is a fair one. I just prefer not to talk about him with you—at least for now. Maybe we will get more personal on our next date."

Awwh shit! She's already deemed me third date worthy. I'm not about to push my luck. I'ma change the subject.

"Fair enough. After dinner do you want to go somewhere to have a drink or two?"

Rachel looked at her watch and frowned. "I'm going to pass on the drinks this time. I have to get home to my daughter. I only paid the sitter to watch her for two hours.

I took care of the bill and we left the restaurant. This time I looked to make sure the coast was clear of any oncoming females. When we arrived at her car Rachel turned and asked, "I noticed you have a slight limp."

"Thanks to you," I replied with a smile.

"I'm sorry about that," Rachel smiled and chuckled. "Now you know what will happen to you if you disrespect me."

I was about to turn and walk away, but Rachel wouldn't let me. She took hold to my elbow and pulled me closer. The heels she wore made her the same height as me. She grabbed my cheek and pulled my head towards her.

The kiss was soft. No tongue. No lip biting. Just a soft peck on my lips designed to give me something to think about. "That's all I get?"

"For now," Rachel whispered. "Handle your business the way you did today and there is more where that came from."

"Fo' sho," I replied, as I stared at her luscious lips. Lord knows I wanted to jack her ass up right there in that parking lot, but I feared for my life. She'd hit me with the car door the last time, I was afraid she might pull out one of those police tasers if I grabbed her.

"Good night, Todd."

"Good night, Rachel."

I left the restaurant feeling like I was walking on clouds. I turned on my radio and started bobbing my head to Prince's hit song *Adore.*

Just as I was about to let my Prince voice kick in and start butchering the man's song, my cell phone rang.

"Hello."

Tee. Tee can you hear me?

"Yeah I can hear you. Who is this?"

It's me… Shakey.

"What's up?"

I'm at the hospital. One of the Emergency Room nurses let me use a phone in one of the empty offices.

"What are you doing at the hospital? It's almost ten o'clock."

I know. Man I broke my foot. I need you to come and get me.

"Which foot did you break? If it's not your right foot then you need to drive yourself home."

I fucked up my left foot. But it doesn't matter because I don't have my car.

"Where's your car?"

Man I left my car outside this little freak's apartment!

"Why?"

Man, I went to Happy Hour at this little hole in the wall bar room and met this chick. She told me she was single and lived alone. When we got to her apartment—which was on the second floor—we started to get busy. All of a sudden I heard somebody bangin' at the front door.

"Let me guess—it was her boyfriend."

Hell yeah! When I asked her who was at the door, she looks at me and says, That's my baby daddy. And he carries a gun.

My boy was in trouble, and I knew it wasn't the right time to start laughing, but I did.

Man this shit aint funny!

"I know, Dog. You're right," I replied as I laughed. "This ain't funny. What happened?"

She got up and let that crazy ma'fucka in.

"What did you do?"

What do you think I did? I jumped out of the dam window.

By this time, I'd pulled my car into a hotel parking lot and was laughing my ass off. Shakey was naturally funny. When he told a story he kept us laughing. This one was the best yet.

"Shakey, you jumped out of a second floor window?"

Hell yeah! That's how I fucked up my ankle. I must have landed wrong or something.

"What happened after that?"

I hopped over to my car and then realized I'd left my car keys on that bitch's coffee table. When I turned around I saw her crazy ass baby daddy coming down the steps. That ma'fucka had a gun in one hand and my car keys in the other hand.

"What did you do?" I asked as I wiped off the tears that were now streaming down my face.

I did the only thing I could do—I hopped away.

"On one leg?"

On one ma'fuckin' leg. I wasn't about to let that nigga kill me.

"Did he run after you?"

He did for a little while. That fool was shouting, Come back and get your keys! *I ain't give a damn about those keys.*

"He couldn't catch you?"

Dog, that nigga couldn't catch me. I was hopping faster than the average nigga can run on two good feet. Man look, I just need you to come and get me. I'll figure out how to get my car later.

After I regained my composure, I went and picked up my crazy-ass friend from the hospital. He was still shaking like a leaf on a tree, but he was alive and that's all that mattered.

It wasn't the way I envisioned my night would end, but it didn't spoil my mood. I was still on a high from the connection I'd made with Rachel. Things were starting to look up.

Two Months Later

24

Rachel

Todd and I had been out several times since that initial dating debacle at the Cheese Cake Factory. I figured it was time he'd finally met my daughter so I invited him over to my place.

Pots and pans were everywhere as I tried to clean up the countertops before Todd arrived. I had to open up my big mouth and brag about my cooking skills. I told him I would cook a nice dinner for him to celebrate his birthday. I even told him to choose the dish. I had no idea he was going to say some of that Louisiana seafood crap.

I'd never even tasted gumbo, but that didn't stop me from messing up my kitchen trying to follow the instructions from the recipe I'd found on the internet.

"Mommy, can I get up?" asked Cupcake from her customary kneeling position in the corner.

I caught her with her hand in the cookie jar—literally. I don't know what I'm going to do with that child. The older she gets the bigger her appetite gets. The bigger her appetite gets the bolder she becomes in her efforts to eat sweets. I could remove all of the sweets from the house, but I don't feel I should have to. I want her to have enough self-discipline to be able to live with her temptations and not act on them.

"No, you stay there for another five minutes."

"But, Mommy, my knees are bleeding!"

"I don't care, that little blood ain't gonna kill you. If you stop disobeying me, you wouldn't have to kneel on the rice."

I never knew it took this long to fix gumbo. And these ingredients are expensive. The recipe required: sausage, okra, gizzards, shrimp, crawfish, crab legs, and bunch of other nasty sounding ingredients. I couldn't find the crawfish and crab legs, so I decided to use just crabmeat instead.

The recipe said I should use gizzards, but I wasn't about to eat any animal's gizzards. I don't even know how gizzards look or taste, but it sounded nasty. I replaced the gizzards with turkey. I've never been a fan of okra. I always thought they became slimy with what looked like snot when cooked. I decided to replace the okra with some asparagus tips I had in the refrigerator.

I figured that once I mixed all that stuff in the pot, Todd wouldn't know the difference anyway. Honestly, I didn't see what all the fuss was about gumbo. The recipe made a big deal about the Roux, but that wasn't that difficult. In my opinion, it looked like a big pot of soup when I finished it. Soup with a bunch of meat piled in it.

I told Todd to come over at 7:30, my doorbell rang at 7:25. He hadn't been late since I checked his ass after our first date.

He's getting trained. Pretty soon I would have him molded exactly the way I wanted him.

"Cupcake, get up upstairs and clean up—you know the routine. Be sure you wipe off your knees real good and put some baby oil on them before you come back down."

"Yes, Ma'am," Cupcake replied as she wiped a tear that was dangling from her cheek.

While Cupcake went upstairs, I tried to fix my hair and clothes. "I'm coming," I shouted.

I ran into my bedroom and examined myself in the six foot tall mirror I had propped up in the corner. The front of my blouse plunged just low enough to show a little cleavage. My breasts were perfectly perky. When I turned to the side I could see that curve all women—well all black women—like to see their assess form in their jeans. I put on some red lipstick and ran to answer the door.

Todd was looking real tasty. His dreadlocks were flawless. He wore a brown blazer and a pair of jeans that hugged his thighs perfectly. I couldn't avoid biting my bottom lip when I snuck a peek at the bulge in his pants.

"Come in," I said and gave him a welcoming hug. That bulge in his pants felt better than it looked when it rubbed up against my leg.

"Hey, Baby," he whispered in my ear. I damn near melted.

We kissed for what seemed like an eternity. It was the most passionate kiss we'd ever shared. Our tongues intertwined like shoe laces. Todd's lips were so soft I could barely feel them. I could feel his hands move from my waist to my ass—I didn't stop them. He cuffed and squeezed. His hands were huge. I surrendered and let him have his way.

I probably would have let him do more if I hadn't heard Cupcake at the top of the staircase.

"Mommy, can I come downstairs?"

"Umm, yeah," I replied as I pulled away from Todd. "Come and meet Mr. Todd."

Cupcake came down the stairs and walked right over to Todd and stuck out her hand.

"Hello, I'm Cupcake."

Todd smiled and shook her hand. "Hello, Cupcake. I'm Todd."

"That's *Mr.* Todd to you," I interjected.

"No sweetheart, you can call me Todd," said Todd.

Cupcake looked up at me. She knew how I disapproved of her referring to adults by their first name.

"My mommy doesn't like for me to call adults by their first name."

"That's right. That's disrespectful," I remarked.

"Well, we're going to make an exception for me. I plan on hanging around here a lot; therefore, it's okay for you to call me Todd."

"Okay," Cupcake replied with a grin.

I was a little taken back by that brief exchange. I wasn't accustomed to anyone undermining my authority—especially when it came to raising my child.

I decided to leave that battle alone—for the time being.

"Come on into the dining room and have seat. Dinner is ready."

"So what are we having?" asked Todd as he pulled out his chair.

"You said you wanted a Creole dish, so I fixed gumbo."

"You actually fixed gumbo? That's a tough dish; especially for someone who wasn't raised in the south or grew up eating it. Those recipes are usually passed down for generations."

"It wasn't that tough. I found a great recipe on the internet. I hope you like it."

You'd better like it. I've spent the last three hours in the kitchen trying to prepare it.

We prayed over the food and started to eat. I could tell from the moment Todd took the first scoop of his gumbo. He stared at the spoon like it had mud on it.

"Is that okra?" he asked.

"No. I can't stand okra so I replaced it with asparagus."

"You put asparagus in gumbo?"

"Yes. Is there a problem?"

"No. No problem. I know that there is no specific way to make gumbo. If you line up five people, you'll probably get five different recipes. I've just never heard of anyone using asparagus."

"Well, there's a first time for everything. Do you eat asparagus?"

"Yes."

"Good."

Todd put the spoon in his mouth and swished the gumbo around. He then reached in his mouth and pulled out the meat.

"This doesn't taste like gizzards."

"That's because it isn't. I replaced the gizzards with turkey. What's wrong?"

Todd shook his head and placed his spoon in his bowl.

"Nothing, Baby. I've just never tasted turkey in gumbo," he replied.

He then turned his attention to Cupcake. Cupcake was examining the gumbo too. She stuck her spoon in her mouth and then spit the gumbo back into the bowl.

"Uggh!" she shouted. "This is nasty!"

Todd started laughing hysterically. "Out of the mouths of babes," he said.

"Cupcake eat your food!" I barked. I tried to hide how offended I was, but my feelings came out.

"But, Mommy it doesn't taste good."

"Cupcake, eat your dinner or else you're going to go to bed hungry."

"Well, Baby, you can't blame her," said Todd. "This is a unique dish."

No this ma'fucka didn't call my meal unique.

"What's that supposed to mean?"

"I didn't mean anything by that, Sweetie. I'm sure there is something else she can eat if she's not feelin' the gumbo."

Livid does not describe how angry I was at that moment. I watched Cupcake use her spoon to move the contents of the bowl around. She was as stubborn as I am. I knew I would have to physically force her to eat it.

"Can I have some cereal?"

"No! You're gonna eat that gumbo!"

"C'mon, Sweetie; give the girl some cereal—it ain't gonna hurt her."

"You don't tell me what to feed my daughter!" I shouted.

Cupcake looked over at Todd like she wanted him to whisk her away and take her to some far off enchanted land. He may have curried favor with her, but he'd pissed me off in the process.

"Get up!" I ordered and grabbed Cupcake by the ear. Twisting her ear was a maneuver I'd inherited from my mother. She used to twist mine when I was young—it was just as effective as a smack.

"Since you don't want to eat what I cooked, you can go to bed on an empty stomach."

I lead Cupcake up to her room, made her put on her night clothes, and get in the bed. Once those missed meal cramps started to kick in, she was going to wish she'd eaten that gumbo.

25

Todd

Rachel had a temper tantrum when Cupcake and I didn't applaud her attempt at making gumbo. Truth be told, that was the worst gumbo I'd ever tasted. The entire time I sat there trying to digest that crap, all I could think about was that old Sugarhill Gang song when they say, *I'm just sitting here making myself nauseous with this ugly food that stinks.*

Rachel's culinary skills may have left a lot to be desired, but that ass looked good in those jeans. It was the first time I'd seen her dressed casually. She usually wore some type of business attire or something a little less revealing when we hooked up. But she was giving me a peek at that voluptuous body that evening. Although I thought her reaction towards Cupcake was over the top, and twisting the child's ear was unnecessarily aggressive, I was okay with her sending Cupcake to bed. I wanted some alone time with Rachel.

When she came back down the stairs I could tell she was frustrated. I figured I could change her disposition if I could get her to lock lips with me again. When I jacked her up at the door, she was definitely letting me have my way with her body.

"Baby, I'm sorry about that," I said as she approached.

I grabbed her elbow and tried to pull her close to me, but she swatted my hand away.

"Don't touch me!" she snapped. "First of all let's get somethin' straight. That is my daughter! If I tell her not to address you by your first name then that's the way it's gonna be until I say otherwise."

Rachel's finger was pressed up against my cheek. I started to tell her to back up and get her hand out of my face, but I didn't want to exacerbate the situation.

"Secondly, it is not your place to undermine my authority by telling her she doesn't have to eat something after I told her she *did* have to eat it."

"You're right, Baby," I said, and tried to grab her elbow again.

"Get your damn hands off of me!" she shouted and then pushed me.

Alright now, you'd better calm your ass down. You may be mad, but don't let your anger write a check your ass can't cash.

"Last but not least, I spent hours in that fuckin' kitchen preparing that gumbo. Even if you didn't like it, you should've had the decency to fake it."

Before I could reply, Rachel had moved towards the front door and opened it.

"So what are you sayin'… you want me to leave?"

"Yes."

"Rachel this is stupid, it's not even that serious. C'mon, Baby. Close the door."

When I reached to close the door, Rachel grabbed my wrist and pulled me towards it. Her fingernails left a huge gash in my skin. A few large welts started to form along parts of my arm and wrist bone.

As I stood with one foot inside the house and the other outside, she reiterated her position.

"I'm not gonna tell you again. Get outta my house! You don't have to worry about me tryin' to do something nice for your ass again!" she shouted and then pushed me completely out the door.

She shoved me so hard that I stumbled. When I regained my balance, I moved towards the door only to have it slammed in my face.

26

Rachel

I've never been so insulted in my life. Here I was trying to bond with him—let him get closer to me—and he comes into my home and insults me. As if hurting my feelings weren't enough, he tried to turn my child against me.

I decided at that moment that Todd wasn't worth the headache. He needed a younger woman—someone he could disrespect and get away with it. Todd was much too rough around the edges for my taste. I needed a man that could assimilate into my world; a man that I could take to dinner engagements and not have to fear that he'd say or do something that would embarrass the heck out of me.

I was feeling a little overwhelmed by my work and personal life so I decided to take a few days of vacation time to get my thoughts together. I needed to pamper myself. A message and spa treatment was overdue.

While sitting in the plush leather chair at my manicurist waiting to be serviced, I decided to open some of the mail that had been sitting in my purse for more than a week. As usual, most of the letters involved Lecar.

People say that you can't hide from you past. I thought they were wrong—until now. Lecar tormented me. Until he was completely gone, I risked losing my daughter, my career, my sanity, and any man that I decided to have a relationship with.

My attorney hadn't done a good enough job of separating my current financial affairs from Lecar. To make matter worse, I had to deal with this asshole who was now blackmailing me. I didn't want to make the payments, but my life could be ruined if I didn't.

As much as I hated to acknowledge it, my only recourse for dealing with being blackmailed was to eliminate the blackmailer. That would solve a big source of my stress. Either eliminate the threat or keep paying for the rest of my life.

My bank account was still looking good, but had taken a hit over the previous three years. My parents both had $200,000 insurance policies on them. After they died, I inherited that money. But between the I.R.S., medical bills from my past life, purchasing my new house here in Atlanta, and paying this extortion, my little nest egg was getting smaller and smaller by the day.

My salary at Boxxmore was more than enough to sustain my lifestyle, but it was time to bring an end to this bullshit. And that's exactly what I intended to do.

Focusing on my financial matters was tough because I couldn't get images of Todd out of my mind. I liked him – more than I wanted to admit. Even Cupcake liked him.

After I put him out she asked about him for two straight days. Within a matter of minutes, he's already won her over. Todd had that kind of affect.

I still maintain that he disrespected me, but the more I thought about it the more I realized that his behavior wasn't a deal breaker. I deliberated whether or not I should call him. I could still feel his touch; the way he cupped and gripped my ass. They way he nibbled on my bottom lip when we kissed. The way he seductively whispered and nibbled on my ear. I hadn't been held like that in years. I wanted him bad - real bad.

Against my better judgment I decided to call him. I was afraid he wouldn't want to see me again after the way I'd kicked him out but my instincts told me he desired me just as badly. That's what my instincts were saying—and that huge bulge in his pants.

27

Todd

Four days passed before I heard from Rachel. I'd resolved that I wasn't going to hear from her again unless I made the first move. The days apart gave me time to think about the dinner episode. The more I thought about it, the more I begin to realize that Rachel had a valid point—actually she'd made a few valid points.

I should not have questioned her parenting; especially in front of the child. The gumbo she'd prepared was terrible, but I should have found a way to guzzle it down. As much as I hated to admit it, I knew I'd been out of line from the moment Cupcake came down those stairs.

The cut she'd left on my wrist was so deep that I had to wrap my wrist. Rachel was too aggressive for my taste. She didn't have a problem inflicting pain on me. The woman needed to take some anger management classes.

Nevertheless, she was due an apology from me, and I was going to give her one. But, first I needed to work on my manuscript. I was close to finishing it, and that four day break from her gave me the uninterrupted time I needed to finish the last chapter.

Once I finished working on my book I needed to track down my shade tree mechanic so that he could take a look at my car. The damn thing kept shutting down on me. It was close to dying, but I wasn't about to spend the money I'd saved on fixing that jalopy. I'd catch the bus if I had to.

With a cup of coffee by my side and a stale donut serving as my fuel, I was in that zone we writers get in. I couldn't be stopped until my cell phone started ringing and I saw Rachel's name displayed on the screen.

"Hello."

Are you busy?

"No, I'm just sitting here writing."

How is the book coming?

"It's coming along. I'm just about finished. Once I complete this last chapter I'll be able to focus on the task of trying to get this thing to the printer."

How are your funds?

"They are coming along. I'm about two thousand short, but I've asked for some more shifts at the club. With the tips I earn, I should be able to round up the money I need in about a month or two."

I wanted to talk to you about that. I'd like to be an investor in your project.

I couldn't believe what I was hearing. The last time I'd spoken to Rachel she was kicking me out of her house. Now she's calling me and offering to invest money in my book. This woman acted like she had split personalities.

I was wondering if you'd come over so that we could talk.

"Umm, that's going to be a problem."

Why?

"Because my car broke down on me. I have to catch up with the guy that fixes it for me."

Maybe it's time to replace it.

"Baby, if I had the money to replace it I would have done that a long time ago. Unfortunately, I'm not rolling in six figures like you and the people you work with. I know you are probably accustomed to dealing with guys that can get their cars fixed the moment a problem pops up, but I'm not in that category—at least not at this moment."

Can you be dressed in and ready to leave in an hour?

"Yeah. Why?"

Just get dressed. I'm coming to pick you up.

"Okay. I'll see you in an hour."

I hung up the phone feeling like Rachel and I were back on. That's the kind of woman I wanted and needed—a take charge chick. That shit was a big turn on for me. I was so accustomed to dealing with women whose finances were worse than mine. Women who rarely paid for dinner. Women who needed a phone bill paid—a car note paid. The chicks I'd dealt with prior to meeting Rachel would have told me to holla at them after I got my car fixed. Not Rachel. Rachel was operating on an entirely different level and I loved it.

Rachel showed up at my apartment around 1:00 o'clock. She was wearing another pair of tight fitting jeans. Her nails were perfectly manicured, her hair was pulled back in a bun, and she was wearing that sexy red lipstick I liked.

"Hey, Baby," she said and then pulled me towards her.

I didn't have a chance to reply because she lodged her tongue in my mouth. I wanted to throw her on the floor and stroke her down right there on the spot.

The scent of her DKNY perfume grabbed hold of my senses and wouldn't let go. Her ass felt even softer than it did a few days earlier. When my body pressed against hers,

I could feel her knot. I'm sure she could feel my manhood pulsating inside of my pants.

I closed the door behind her and pressed her body against the door. "I'm glad you came over, Baby. I don't want to fight."

"Neither do I," she purred.

"I want you, Baby," I said, I didn't care if it sounded like I was begging.

"I want you too… but not now," she replied. "I didn't come here for sex. I came here to apologize for my behavior the other day. I feel strongly about what I said, but I shouldn't have snapped the way I did. It was wrong of me to make you leave."

"You mean put me out," I said and smiled.

"Yes; put you out," she said and chuckled. "I shouldn't have shoved you like that. Do you forgive me?"

"Of course I do. I earned that shove. I don't want to dwell on that. Let's move on."

"I agree. I want to start moving on by surprising you."

"What do you have in mind?"

"Come with me and you'll see."

We left my apartment and drove a few miles until we arrived at the Jaguar dealership. It was the same dealership that Rachel's party was held at. I wasn't sure why we'd gone there, but by the time we parked I did.

A well dressed sales rep approached the car.

"Rachel, I'm glad you came."

"I told you I was," she replied. "This is my boyfriend, Todd. Todd this is John—he's going to let you look at a few of their used Jaguars."

"What?" I replied. "Are you serious?"

"She's very serious," John replied. "Follow me."

As the three of us walked towards the lot where they kept the previously owned Jaguars, I whispered in Rachel's ear, "Baby you know I can't afford any of these cars."

"Don't worry about it—I got you," she replied. "I bought my car from this dealership. I've also sent several customers to him so he owes me a favor."

"Baby, I'm flattered—I really am. But, I can't let you do this. These cars are too expensive."

"Todd, I told you I have it under control. I'm going to take care of the down payment. You're going to have to pay the car note, but it shouldn't be that much. I'll help you with that too."

"What if I can't make the payment?"

"Then I will personally repossess the car. I'm not going to let you ruin my credit. Besides, I trust you will do the right thing."

"Baby, I don't know about this."

"Todd, you need transportation. That car you have is a money trap. The money you spend getting it fixed every few weeks would cover a few car notes."

"That's true," I replied.

"You need reliable transportation. If I had the hook up at a Ford dealership we would go there, but I don't—my hook up is here. That *should* make you smile."

Make me smile was an understatement. I was grinning like a sissy at a Construction Worker convention. Two hours later, I was driving off that lot driving in a 1998 Emerald Green, X-Type Jaguar. I don't know how much money she put down as down payment, but my note was only three hundred dollars.

My boys ain't gonna believe this shit. They're gonna freak out when they see me in this car.

"Follow me!" Rachel shouted out of the window.

I followed her to a nearby restaurant where we had a hearty meal and drinks. I was on cloud nine. I couldn't tell if what I was feeling was love or infatuation. Whatever it was, it had a hold of my heart like a vice grip.

While eating dinner, Rachel told me that she was going to pay for the first print run of my novel. When I told her it would cost nearly three thousand dollars, she didn't blink an eye. She simply smiled and said, "Don't worry, Baby. I got you."

After our meal, Rachel and I went back to my apartment. When we got inside, the lust fest continued. The intensity was heightened once she allowed me to back her into my bedroom.

Rachel kicked off her shoes and got in my bed. I went into my bathroom and pulled out my box of condoms.

Finally, she's gonna give me some ass. I need to calm down because I'm too excited right now. If I cum too fast I may not get another shot at the coochie. Hell, she may even take the damn car back. I need to be at my absolute best. C'mon Tee, get yourself together. Take a deep breathe. Be cool. This ain't your first piece of ass. You're the man. You're known for breaking chicks off. She's just another woman.

My pep talk to myself worked. I calmed down a little, but I needed this evening to go well—extremely well.

I reached inside of my medicine cabinet and grabbed a little bottle of ginseng that I kept in case of emergencies and this moment definitely qualified as an emergency. I swallowed the capsule, took a swig of mouthwash, swished around in my mouth and then spit it out. I was feeling refreshed when I re-entered my room.

I expected to see Rachel undressed and eager to receive a vaginal beat down, but she wasn't. Rachel was lying on the bed with her back towards me.

I nestled behind her and immediately slid my hand under the back of her shirt. My fingers made their way to her bra strap. Just as I was about to hit her with my patented thumb and index finger bra release technique, she reached around and grabbed my hand.

"Stop Todd."

"What's wrong?" I asked. I figured her back was hurting from the tip of my rock hard dick pressed against her.

"I'm not ready for this," she replied softly.

"What do you mean? You seem ready to me."

"Todd, I wasn't playing when I told you I didn't believe in casual sex. When I give myself to a man I want him to be my husband."

I was shocked. I couldn't believe what she was saying. I didn't know how to respond. While I searched for a reply I swear I heard my penis talking to me.

Tell her what she wants to hear fool! Tell her you want to be her husband. Tell her you'll fly to Las Vegas today. Say something—me and your balls need some pussy.

"Uhhh, I feel you. Maybe we need to get engaged or something."

"What?" Rachel asked.

My mind was telling me to pull up, but my penis was telling me to keep the bullshit flowing.

"I mean, seriously, Baby—we've experienced more in these last few months than some couples experience in years. As of today we are even sharing our finances to a certain degree."

"Todd, are you serious? This isn't a topic to play with."

Her ass felt so soft. My manhood was lodged right between the crack of her ass. I would have agreed to sleep with Sadam Hussein at that moment if it would have earned me two or three deep strokes.

"I'm dead serious. We should get engaged. When two people are feeling each other emotionally, you can't put a time frame on love."

"Todd, are you saying you love me?" Rachel asked, and then caressed my ear lobe.

"Yeah. Yeah, Baby. That's what I'm saying," I replied as my eyes rolled in the back of my head from her sensitive touch.

Rachel turned around and faced me. She grabbed my face with her hands and kissed me softly.

"Todd, I'm 40 years old. I don't want to play games. I'm ready to settle down. I think you and I have something special here. I want to spend my life with you."

"I feel the same way, Baby."

"I promise you sweetie. The day we say *I do*, I'm going to give you everything you want."

"Everything?"

"Baby I'm going to sex your brains out. I promise you… it will be worth the wait."

We spent the next few hours spooning in my bed. I'd started the day broke, without transportation, and as far as I knew, without a girlfriend. I ended the day, driving a new car, having enough money to pay for the printing of my book, and engaged.

Even I couldn't have developed a storyline that would have rivaled this chain of events.

28

Kim

Todd and Rachel have been dating each other for more than two months now. I never thought I'd say this, but I'm glad they are. I don't know what he's been doing to her—and I really don't want to know—but whatever it is, it's working.

Not only did Rachel keep me as her Administrative Assistant, she even agreed to put me in the company's Management Development Program. I'm scheduled to start in a few months and I can't wait.

Everything is flowing smoothly—everything except my relationship with Todd. He's been bugging me for weeks to meet him for lunch so that we can talk about our issues, but I've been making excuses to avoid the topic. I figured it was about time to get it over with so I agreed to meet him.

We met at a Panera Bread Bakery near our apartments. On Saturday mornings, Panera is packed with people and this day was no different. Old white couples were stationed wall-to-wall sipping on coffee and gumming down bagels. Todd stood out like a sore thumb.

"Over here!" he shouted as he waved.

I started to pretend I didn't see him, but it was too late. The moment we made eye contact he started waving like he was at a Mardi Gras parade.

"Hey, Sis. I already ordered us some breakfast."

"How do you know what I want?"

"I ordered you one of those Cinnamon Crunch bagels. Everybody likes those. I even got you some coffee. I wasn't sure how you liked it spiked so I rounded up a few packs of this Equal and cream."

"Cool. You're lookin' happy these days."

"Yeah, ya boy is feelin' good. I just finished my novel. Rachel and I are starting to get closer. Everything is good."

"So you and Rachel are actually getting tight. I still can't believe that you are dating my boss."

"Yeah, we've been kickin' it. I really like her. She could be the one."

I nearly spit my coffee out. I couldn't believe what I was hearing. Todd is talking about marrying my boss. That's like Lil Wayne marrying Oprah.

"Excuse me?"

Todd started laughing. "You heard me. I said I think Rachel is wifey material."

"Todd, you just met her a few months ago. You need to slow your roll. You're gonna scare her off."

"How am I gonna scare her off and she's the one who brought up the topic first?"

That time I *did* spit out my coffee. It went up my nose, down my chin, and on my blouse.

"Damn, Girl. You act like you don't know how to drink out of a cup."

That coffee was so hot it felt like it nearly singed my nose hairs. I grabbed a napkin and dabbed my shirt as I tried to wrap my mind around Todd's remarks. Was he actually suggesting that Rachel proposed to him after only knowing him for a little over two months?

I was about to ask him to elaborate, but I was distracted by the bandage around his wrist.

"Boy, what happened to your wrist?"

"What, this little scratch? I just wrapped it up so that it wont get infected."

"The way you have it wrapped, it must be more than a little scratch."

"Me and the fellas were playin' basketball. Big Bubba accidentally scratched me."

"Damn, I'd hate to see how you'd look if he intentionally hit you. Anyway, back to your comment. Did you say that Rachel proposed to you?"

"She didn't actually propose, but she did ask me how I felt about marriage and made it very clear to me that she wasn't interested in casual dating. She told me that she was only going to continue to date me if I was interested in marriage."

"I don't believe this. Does she think her biological clock is ticking or something?"

"I don't know. I was just as shocked as you are. But the more I thought about it, the more I started to warm up to the idea. I'm tired of one night stands. I want to be in a relationship that's based on something more than sex."

"Sounds like you've been turned out by an older woman."

"Shiiiit, your lil brother could never get turned out by any woman. As a matter of fact, Rachel and I have never slept together. She made it clear I couldn't have any until we were married."

"And you're still hanging around? You must be sick."

"I know. I've surprised myself. I've never waited more than two weeks to smash a chick, but when I'm with Rachel I don't even think about it. I'm fallin' for her mind. Don't get it twisted; I'll smash her if she lets me. But, it hasn't come to that."

"T.M.I.—I don't want to know about y'all sex life. I'm just trippin' off of everything you've said."

"I know. This shit is crazy."

"Have you even met or spent time with her daughter?"

"Of course. Me and Cupcake are tight."

"She let's you call her daughter Cupcake?"

"Yep."

"Damn, she must really be feelin' yo ass. Well, what do you know about her ex-husband?"

"I know he's an asshole. I know he's threatened to take Danielle back to Africa."

"What are you gonna do if he comes around starting some shit?"

"What do you think I'ma do? I'ma handle my business."

"Todd, you don't need to be getting involved in some pre-existing drama."

"Kim, I'm a big boy. I can handle myself. Besides, I intend to be there for Rachel because she's been there for me."

"What do you mean by that? Y'all have only been dating for a few months."

"It's only been a few months, but she puts her money where her mouth is," Todd replied and then turned around and pointed at his car parked outside. "You see that car out there?"

"Which one?"

"That green Jaguar," Todd replied, with a grin as wide as the Mississippi River.

"Yeah, what about it?"

"It's mine. Rachel hooked me up with after my car broke down a few days ago."

"You're lying!"

"No I'm not. I'm as serious as a heart attack. You know it was my birthday last week and you didn't even call me—but that's cool. Anyway, my car broke down last week. Since my birthday was one week away, she bought that used Jag. We got it from that same dealership where y'all had that party. I think she knows the owner or something. They gave her the hook up."

"I don't care what the occasion was or that the car is used. That is an expensive gift. When a woman does something like that for a man, she is playing for keeps."

"That's cool. I told you I'm ready to settle down. That's not all."

"There's more?"

"Well, Rachel has offered to help me publish my novel."

"What?"

"You heard me. Rachel's gonna invest two thousand dollars in my project. She's also helping me with the paperwork so that I can set up a publishing company—you have to set up one if you're going to self-publish."

"Wait, wait, wait…slow your roll. You can't be serious?"

"I'm very serious. Stay tuned. You might be working for your sister-in-law by this time next year. You shouldn't be complaining, you are going to benefit from this too."

"How? Is she gonna buy me a Jaguar too?"

"No. But if I'm not mistaken, you were just told that you were being placed in the Management Development Program."

"Yeah, what's your point?"

"My point is—you should be thanking me instead of hatin' on me. Your little brother is the person who convinced Rachel to put you into that program."

"No, my work performance got me into that program."

"I don't doubt that your work performance would have eventually got you into the program, but the fact that your boss is dating me, didn't hurt."

Todd's words cut me to my core. I didn't want his help. I didn't ask for his help. And I didn't believe I needed his help. I worked my ass off during my tenure at Boxxmore; if that wasn't enough to get me into that program then I didn't want it.

I rolled my eyes at him so hard it hurt my eye sockets. I could tell by the look in his eyes that he knew I was about to unleash my wrath.

"Look here, Sis; before you start getting all pissed off, you need to know that I was only trying to help you out."

I wanted to wrap my hands around his neck and choke the shit out of him. He was still the little arrogant and cocky son-of-a-bitch I remembered as a child.

"First of all, I didn't ask for your damn help! Secondly, if you wanna help me why don't you…"

"Why don't I do what? Finish your comment. I know it's gonna be something negative. Nigga tried to help you out, and all you do is bitch and complain. If it wasn't for me, you would be making coffee and fetching donuts for another six months."

That was all I needed to hear. I lit into his ass like we were the only people in that bakery.

"…you can help me by acknowledging what you did!"

"I've already admitted that I spoke to Rachel on your behalf."

"I'm not talkin' about that jackass! I'm talkin' about the hurtful things you said to me ten years ago."

Todd looked at me like I was an alien. He literally tilted his head the way dogs do when they are trying to figure out what we humans are trying to say.

"Ten years ago? Girl, we're talkin' bout what's goin' on now. Stop living in the past!"

"Yes, ten years ago. Do you need me to refresh your memory?" I asked rhetorically. "I will. I'm talking about the hurtful things you said to me after your trifling-ass daddy killed my mama!"

Suddenly, the busy bakery became silent. It was like the old EF Hutton commercials. I was talking and everybody in the bakery stopped to listen. The old couple sitting in the booth a few feet away from us, put their newspapers on the table and were watching us like we were actors in a damn movie.

"You need to calm your ass down," said Todd.

But it was too late for reasoning with me. His condescending attitude mixed with the still fresh memory of his mean spirited remarks, created an anger more harmful than acid. At that very moment I hated him, and I didn't care who knew it.

"I don't need to do a damn thing! You need to apologize for what you said to me."

"What?"

"Don't play stupid Todd. You never apologized to me for saying that I caused mama to die."

Todd just sat there for a moment. I could see the wheels turning in his head. I expected him to get up and walk out, but he didn't. He fired back at me.

"If the shoe fits, wear it."

I was stunned. He didn't blink. He stared right at me. His face lacked emotion. His eyes squinted and his pupils seemed to get smaller – like two little dark brown dots. For a moment I thought I was sitting across from the devil.

Todd meant what he said to me ten years earlier when were in the counselor's office, and he meant it now as we sat in that crowded bakery. From the look on his face and the tone in his voice, he meant it even more.

29

Rachel

"Lance, if you tell me to calm down one more time I'm gonna fire you right here on the spot."

Well Rachel, I guess you're going to have to fire me because I am going to tell you to calm down. Getting emotional isn't going to change things.

My staff and I have done all we can to protect you—and I think we've done a damn good job up until this point. We've cleared your name of many of the pending debt issues, and erased any traces of your whereabouts. But, the fact remains that you are going to have to change your last name and pay some of these outstanding debts to lessen the chances of being found. If you don't these collection accounts are going to be turned over to litigation.

"No shit, Sherlock."

Some of these companies will hire investigators to track you down. I suggest you cash in some of your stock options and empty a few accounts to come up with about $40,000 so that you can pay these last two debts.

"If I do this, will I no longer have to deal with this Lecar shit again?"

I believe so. Once those two debts are taken care of, you should be in the clear.

"How do I deal with this extortion issue?"

I have told you to go to the cops.

"And I told you that I can't do that. If I go to the police it's going to expose me to more inquiries."

Well, all I can say to you is to keep paying and hope that the situation goes away.

I hung up the phone without saying good-bye. Every time I think I'm free from Lecar and all the bullshit surrounding him, something new pops up.

I drove to Jonesboro to exchange a pair of shoes I'd purchased from a specialty shop for Cupcake a week earlier. My head was pounding and I was starving. My instincts told me to take I-285 so that I could avoid the downtown traffic, but I didn't listen to them. Since the specialty store was located at an exit off of I-75, I decided to stay on the city's main artery—bad decision.

30

Todd

It had been nearly two weeks since Kim and I made a scene in that bakery. I'd spent a lot of time reflecting on the argument, and I still didn't feel bad about what I said. As far as I was concerned she had it coming. Every since we reconnected I'd tried to be cordial and loving towards her, but she's the one who was acting standoffish.

I had a dream the other night. Calling it a dream is an understatement—it was actually a nightmare. I usually have two or three a month.

In this reoccurring nightmare I find myself standing in the living room of the house Kim and I grew up in. I'm fighting my dad after I walk in on him beating my mom. While he and I are fighting, Kim is sitting on the sofa watching television. She refuses to help me fight him. All she says in my dream is, *He's your daddy—you deal with him.*

The dream always ends the same way, he punches me in the face and I fall to the floor. He then grabs my mother by her hair and drags her into the bedroom. The entire time all this is happening, Kim continues to sit on the sofa watching television. While she's watching television and I'm on the floor, we can hear the sound of smacks and clothes being ripped coming from my parent's bedroom.

I usually wake up from my dream around that time. Most of the time my shirt and bed sheets are soaking wet and tears are streaming down my face. The dream never changes and neither does my response.

It was these haunting dreams and memories that made it hard for me to apologize to Kim for accusing her of being the cause of our mother's death. As much as I want to take back what I said I can't. To do so would be disingenuous. A part of me really feels that if she would have acted a little faster my mother would still be alive. As a matter of fact, I believe she owes my mother and me an apology. She's never once told me she was sorry for not doing more.

I know some people would feel I should give Kim the benefit of the doubt. I should understand that she was in some form of shock. She feared for her life. She's a girl and I'm a boy; therefore, it was okay for her to be frightened, but not me.

Well that's bullshit! I was scared that horrible night... probably more than her. She's always bragging about her independence and determination, but where was all that determination when it was needed the most?

I refused to make another attempt at reconciliation. As far as I was concerned, if Kim didn't reach out to me, we weren't going to ever talk again.

I got a call from Bubba asking me to pick up his little sister from the airport. She was coming to town to hang with him for a few days. Bubba was stuck at the dentist office, and couldn't get away.

Bubba's sister Tangy was a twenty-two year old dime piece. She was the biggest flirt known to man, and wouldn't you know it—she had a crush on me. I really didn't want to go get her because I knew she would extend an offer to let me tap that ass. Every time she offered to rock my world I found it harder and harder to refuse.

Tangy came out of the airport terminal and stood on the sidewalk. I was parked a few feet away in my car. She didn't notice me stationed a few feet away. Tangy had one of those ghetto booties. The type that jiggled whenever she moved. Shit, Tangy's booty jiggled whenever she breathed. The only reason why I hadn't already screwed her brains out was because she was my best friend's little sister.

I pulled up beside her and yelled out the window, "What's up, Tangy. I see you out here posing."

"Todd!" she shouted.

I got out of the car and walked around to the sidewalk to pick up her luggage. Tangy literally jumped into my arms. I'm sure the people walking past thought we were a couple.

When Tangy jumped into my arms, I caught her—my first mistake. My hands instinctively grabbed her ass. I had two handfuls of the softest cheeks I'd ever felt in my life.

"I'm sorry," I said as I quickly removed my hands. When I let go of her, her feet landed on the ground and she released her bear hug.

"Whatever! You know you meant to do that," she said and blushed.

"No, I didn't. I'm sorry."

"Don't apologize. You don't hear me complaining."

"Tangy, don't play with me. I'm a grown-ass man."

"And I'm a grown-ass woman! You don't believe me, ask your hands—I'm sure they will vouch for me."

"Girl, get in the car," I said out loud. In my mind all I could think was, *Lord, give me the strength I need to not bend her fine ass over and give her what she wants.*

I made it from the airport to Bubba's apartment in fifteen minutes—it's normally a twenty five to thirty minute drive. I needed to get Tangy out of my car as soon as possible. I was starting to get weak. I hadn't had sex in nearly five months. Rachel wasn't giving me any sex, and the lack of sex - and subsequent infrequent ejaculation - made my testicles seem the size of a bell pepper.

I'd been successful at my first attempt at monogamy, and I didn't want to ruin it—especially with someone like Tangy.

"Well, we're here," I said as I hopped out of the car and retrieved her luggage from the back seat.

Tangy had her key chain on her index finger and was twirling it around.

"You know you are welcome to come in for a little while."

"Nah, I'd better not. Bubba should be home soon."

"No he won't. He's got to go to the club for a meeting after he leaves the dentist," Tangy replied, and then moved closer to me.

We were standing inches apart. I was growing weak.

Lord, I thought you were going to help a brotha out?

"Nawh, I'm gonna bounce."

"Are you sure?" Tangy asked and then reached down and squeezed my dick. She gripped the head of my penis and then cupped my balls. I wasn't expecting that. She caught me and my balls off guard. I actually squirted in my pants.

With my balls secured in her hand, Tangy leaned over and softly kissed my lips. She used her free hand to grab my shirt and pull me closer as she whispered in my ear, *"I won't tell a soul. I just wanna fuck you one time. My pussy is calling you."*

I was so turned on and surprised by her advance that I started stuttering, "Ooooh no. No no no. I… I got… I gotta… gotta go."

I found the strength to pull away from Tangy's grip and jumped in my car. I sped off and left her ass standing right there on the sidewalk. I survived her advances. I needed to go home and change my drawers. But, I was proud of myself.

I went home and took a cold shower and jacked off. After pleasuring myself, I got in the bed and took a nap. It was three o'clock in the afternoon, and I had to be at the club at eight o'clock. I needed to get some rest before I tackled the city's Saturday night party goers.

My nap lasted nearly three hours. I was butt naked and wrapped up in my covers as I lay in my bed in the fetal position. That was the best nap I'd had in months. I probably would have slept another hour if I hadn't heard my phone ringing.

"Hello," I said in a voice that was so deep and groggy that I probably sounded like Barry White.

"Hey," said Rachel. Her sweet voice had a way of injecting life into me.

"Hey, Baby. What's up?"

"What time are you going to work?"

"I have to be there around eight o'clock. What time is it?" I asked, struggling to gather my senses.

"It's a little after six. I need you to swing by my house on your way to work. I wanna give you something before you head in."

"What you got for me?"

"You'll see when you get here."

"Okay. I'll be there in an hour."

"Great. I love you."

Damn I loved to hear her say that. She first told me she loved me after our sixth date. When she first said it I took a double take. We'd only kissed a few times up until that point, so to hear her say those words shocked me. Rachel is always so serious. Stoic. When she broke down and told me that she was falling in love with me, I felt like melting. I told her I was falling in love with her too—although I didn't really mean it. Now I believe I do.

"I love you too, Baby."

The lights in Rachel's living room were turned off. As I walked up the walkway towards her front door, I could see a note taped to her front door.

The front door is unlocked. Come inside, place your keys on the counter and put the blind fold that's sitting on the counter, over your eyes.

My heart rate sped up. I could hear my heart thumping inside my chest. I opened the door and could hear the sweet sounds of Miles Davis playing on the radio. The scent of jasmine lingered in the air and infiltrated my nostrils.

I walked over to the counter and placed my keys down. I picked up the blind fold and covered my eyes. Once I put that blind fold over my eyes, I felt like I was suspended in a deep black hole.

I stood in the same spot for a few second before I heard Rachel's voice from behind.

"I'm glad you came," she said and then pressed her body against my back. Her hands moved up and down my chest and then danced around my crotch.

"What's all this?"

"This is what you've earned," Rachel replied, and then used her hands to undo my belt buckle. She pulled my belt off and unbuttoned the top button of my pants.

"Turn around," she whispered.

I did as I was told as my pants dropped to my ankles and my dick stretched out like Pinocchio's nose.
Suddenly the lights came on.

"Take off your blind fold," Rachel commanded. I lifted the blind fold from around my eyes just in time to see her fist flying towards my eye.

Rachel hit me so hard I swear I saw stars. I'd been in fights with guys who couldn't hit that hard. I flipped over the high back chair that was positioned two feet away, and landed on my ass.

"What the fuck's going on?" I shouted.

"You wanna know what's going on? Okay, I'll tell you what's going on. I was in Clayton County today. I saw you riding around with some bitch in the car I bought you. That's what's going on you bastard!"

I could feel my left eye swelling. It was filled with water and hurt like heck. I was hopping around trying to get my balance, but my pants were tangled around my ankles. I used my right hand to try and pull up my pants while I covered my eye with my left, but that shit wasn't working. I suspect I was looking like Shakey after he jumped out that second floor window.

"I didn't tell you to get up!" Rachel shouted, and then struck me across the stomach with the buckle of my belt. I immediately knew how Kunta Kinte felt when those slave masters beat his ass.

I fell to my knees. I didn't remain on my knees long because a series of punches to my face and head left me in the fetal position on the floor. A vase flew past my head hitting the fireplace, and I could hear glass shattering.

It seemed like she beat me for an eternity. Once the blows stopped, I remained curled up—I wasn't sure if she was just taking a break. It wasn't until I heard my car keys shaking that I felt at ease. I slowly stood and pulled up my pants.

"I tried to support your ass. I tried to help you out and you do this to me."

"I didn't do anything! That was Bubba's little sister. She's like a sister to me."

"Oh really? Since when does your sister grab your dick?"

Oh shit! She must have followed us to Bubba's apartment.

"Baby, I swear I didn't know she was gonna do that. You saw me leave her standing there."

"You should have never put yourself in that position!" Rachel shouted and then slapped me across the head again.

I could taste blood in my mouth. I wasn't sure if it was coming from my lips, my tongue, or both. She clenched her fist and prepared to swing at me again. I don't know what came over me, but I was determined to stop being her punching bag.

Rachel cocked her arm back. If my face was New York, the punch she threw at me came from Louisiana. It swept through Alabama; picked up speed in Georgia; blew through the east coast like a hurricane; and hit my face harder than the worst winter snow storm.

I could feel my teeth rattle from the impact. I staggered backwards a few steps and then leaned against the wall. I could hear her heels clacking on the floor as she walked towards me. When she got within a few inches I transformed from that punching bag to Mike Tyson.

"That's the last time I'm gonna let you get away with hitting me," I shouted as I charged at Rachel and grabbed her neck.

I could see the look of surprise in Rachel's eyes. She looked like the bully who was finally punched once in the face by the school's nerd. I had such a strong grip on her throat that I could have probably yanked her vocal chords out and dangled them in her face.

The force of my charge sent both of us reeling. I don't know how we made it cross the room, but when we stopped, Rachel's back was pressed up against her living room window. It's a miracle the window didn't break into a thousand pieces when we hit it.

"I told you I didn't do anything," I shouted and then cocked back my fist. I was aiming to give her a nice healthy dose of her own medicine.

Just as I was about to unleash a can of whip ass on Rachel, I caught a flashback to my childhood. Two scenes dominated my memory at that moment: the night my father had my mother suspended in mid air as he choked her; and my mother's last words as she lay dying in my arms.

The scene was surreal. It was like I was having an out of body experience. I looked around Rachel's living room. Glass was everywhere. The curtains on the window I had Rachel pressed up against had fallen on the floor. I could see the neighbor's house. Unfortunately for us, the neighbors could see us too.

I released my grip on Rachel's neck. A sense of shame came over me. I could see my mother's beautiful face looking down at me from heaven. I started to mumble, "I didn't break my promise, Mama. I didn't break my promise."

My trance was broken when I heard Rachel's voice, "Get the fuck outta my house. And I'm taking these car keys. You ain't gonna use a car that I bought so that you can ride around town with your little funky-ass girlfriends."

"How am I gonna get to work?"

"I don't give a damn if you make it to work or not," she said as she walked into her bedroom and slammed the door.

I spent the next two or three minutes fixing my clothes. I bent down to pick up my belt from off the floor, and felt one of the worse pains I'd ever experienced. The side of my body felt like it was tearing open every time I moved.

I was hesitant to do it, but I finally found the nerve to raise my shirt and examine the spot where my belt buckle struck. Rachel hit me so hard that it left an imprint on my rib cage.

I eventually left Rachel's. With a torn shirt and bruised face and body, I had to decide whether or not to go to work or back to my apartment. My wallet wanted me to go to work and earn some money, but my body was yearning to soak in a hot tub.

Whichever option I chose, I'd have to catch the bus or a cab to get there. I started walking towards the entrance to Rachel's subdivision. I was about to turn the corner when I noticed flashing lights approaching from behind.

The strobe light mounted on the door of the police car was blinding. The police officers driving the car weren't moved by my attempts to block the light from my eyes.

"Sir, stop right there," shouted one of the officers as he got out of the car—his right hand positioned on his gun holster.

I may have been in agony, but I wasn't delirious. Every black man in America knows that when the cops pull up on you, you can either run or you can follow their instructions and remain standing in the same spot.

It's a catch 22 because you learn early in life that being brutalized by the police at some point in your life is almost a certainty—to some degree it's a right of passage.

The rule of thumb in is to sit your ass on that curb, to minimize the brutality. Running from the cops will surely lead to an emergency room visit and a few stitches.

"What's up officer's," I replied.

"We received a report that a couple was fighting."

The neighbors must have called the police. I couldn't even get mad at them. The sight of Rachel and me fighting after we knocked down the curtains must have been horrifying.

"Uhhh, it's nothing. My girlfriend and I had a little argument."

"That's not how it was reported, Sir," said the cop that got out of the passenger side of the police cruiser. "Get down on the ground!" he shouted.

The officer pounced on my back and slapped the handcuffs on me. Where is your girlfriend, Sir?"

"She's back at her house. She lives at 2213 Fairview."

"Did you assault your girlfriend sir?"

"Uhhh, no it's not like that. If anything, all I did was try to defend myself."

"Are you saying your girlfriend attacked you?"

Damn, I ain't tryin' to snitch on my own woman, but I don't know what else to do. These cops are ready to take my ass to jail and they haven't even heard the whole story.

"Officer, all I'm sayin' is that we had a little argument and she got upset. She thought I was messing with another woman, and she lost her cool."

"So there was a fight?"

"Uhhh, no—I mean, yeah. I mean, somethin' like that—it wasn't serious."

"Let's take him back to the house and speak to the woman," said one officer to the other.

They shoved me into the back seat of the police cruiser and drove back to Rachel's house. The officers got out of the car and approached Rachel's front door. I had no idea what Rachel was going to say, but considering how mad she was, there was no telling how far under the bus she was going to throw me.

I started to get more nervous the longer the officer's stood at the front door. I was glad to see that Rachel didn't let them inside because the sight of that living room would have surely bought me a one-way ticket to jail.

The officer's walked back to the cruiser. One of them actually had a smirk on his face. They got in the car and commenced to humiliating me.

"Well sir, we spoke to Ms. Biko. It seems that you were telling the truth. She admitted to being the aggressor."

"Yeah, she looks like she was real aggressive," said the other office and chuckled.

"What did you do to upset that woman like that?"

"I didn't do anything. She has a bad temper. She thought I was seeing another woman and she lost her cool."

"She thought you were seeing another woman?" asked one of the officers in a mocking tone. "That's your story and you are sticking to it?"

"That's right. She thought I was with another woman, but I wasn't."

"Yeah right," replied the second officer, clearly disinterested in this case."

"Look Sir, technically you have the right to press charges against her. After all, she did admit to being the aggressor."

"I'm not tryin' to send my woman to jail," I said.

"Yeah, that's not a good look," said one of the officers. "Especially if you know your actions provoked the incident. If I were you I'd take that whipping like a man and go home and sleep it off."

"Yeah, give her a day or so and she'll be over it—at least that's how my wife handles it," said the second cop as they both started laughing.

The officers took the handcuffs off of me and then brought me home. My body was transported to my residence, but my pride was left somewhere on Fairview Street.

I spent the night on my sofa. Trying to sleep with bruised ribs was very uncomfortable, but I managed to get a few hours of shut eye. The clock was just about to strike eight o'clock when I rolled over the next morning. Darkness prevailed throughout my tiny apartment, but I could hear the ticking of the wall-mounted clock a few feet away.

"Man I don't believe this shit," I mumbled. "Rachel didn't seem like herself."

With my head propped up on a sofa pillow, I laid there staring up at the ceiling. Images of my childhood dominated my thoughts. I never thought I'd end up the victim of domestic violence, but that's the situation I found myself in.

I started wondering how I could have avoided this. I questioned my response: should I have let Rachel get all of her frustration out or should I have fought back. I even wondered if I should break up with her after witnessing her anger.

When you experience a traumatic incident like I'd gone through, it's only natural that you recall past life experiences—the ones you try to bury deeply. While enveloped in darkness, I did just that—reminisced.

One scene in particular kept coming to mind—a scene that took place long before my father killed my mother. It happened late one night when Kim and I were probably around six and eight years old. We lived in a two bedroom, rat infested, shotgun style house. The entire house was probably less than 1,000 square feet, but back then it seemed long and huge to me.

Kim and I had to share the same bed. My parent's room was on the other side of the wall. It must have been after midnight and the house was as silent as a tomb—until I heard the ruckus.

My sister was sound asleep, but I was wide awake. To this day I wish I could have switched places with her.

"No Kennedy," I heard my mother whisper.

"Woman you don't tell me no," my dad replied. The sound of his voice still sends chills through me.

There was a struggle taking place. I could hear their sheets rustle and my mother's helpless pleas for him to stop. At first her voice was audible and then her voice sounded muffled. Always trying to protect her kids from the harsh realities of her life, she suffered in silence—even while she was being violated.

The sound of someone being smacked echoed through the night and then the disturbing sound of my father panting and grunting. I closed my eyes and tried hard to get to that unconscious state that Kim and I often escaped to.

It wasn't until years later that I realized what happened to my mother that night—and many other nights. She was being raped by her own husband.

Images of him placing a pillow over her head consumed me along with the nagging question; how could a man rape the woman he was supposed to love?

I spent my entire life trying not to be like him. My mother didn't have to insist that I promise to never hit a woman; by the time she was killed by my father, I already knew about the abuse she'd experienced and the emotional impact it had on her—I just never told her.

Hitting a woman was never an option for me, and I was angry at myself for engaging in that tussle with Rachel. I was dealing with the realization that I no longer had transportation. The motor on my car was shot. Rachel made it clear that I wasn't allowed to drive the Jaguar. I was fucked and I knew it. I wouldn't have any way to make it to my two jobs without that car. Shit, after missing work without calling in, I may no longer have my bartending job at the club.

As ridiculous as it may sound, I even wondered whether or not I should apologize to her. I'd never chased a woman before, but the fact of the matter was, I needed Rachel. I needed her emotionally and financially.

"I wonder if she's going to help me with my book," I said in a low tone. "Shit, I'm screwed."

Thoughts of my financial predicament were interrupted by a vision of my friends finding out. How in the heck was I going to explain these bruises to them? They were going to rib me for weeks once they saw the condition I was in. It would be nice if I had the type of friends I could confide in, but I don't. Bubba is about the most sensible one out of the bunch, but I don't even want to tell him about this.

By the time the clock on the wall read 9 o'clock I was wide awake. I managed to get off the sofa long enough to use the bathroom.

While in the bathroom I heard a knock at my door.

"Shit! Who is that this early in the morning?"

I looked through the peep-hole and saw a blonde hair white man wearing a goofy looking hat on the other side.

"I have a flower delivery for Todd Wayne," said the guy.

"Yeah, I'm Todd. Thanks."

The guy handed me a huge bouquet of yellow roses. They were in a large vase, and were in full bloom. I placed the flowers on my kitchen table and read the card attached.

Baby I'm sorry about last night. I know I overreacted. Please forgive me.

Luv, Rachel

P.S.
Look outside. You left something at my house. The keys are underneath the driver side floor mat.

I read the card at least ten times before I went downstairs and grabbed the car keys. Suddenly my bruises didn't hurt as much. A warm feeling came over me. "This woman really loves me."

After returning upstairs with my keys in hand and the feeling that everything was going to be okay after all, I started to fix a pot of coffee. Just as I was pouring a cup of my favorite Brazilian blend, there was another sound of banging at my door.

"Todd, open the door fool. We know you're in there?" someone shouted in a husky tone.

That can't be anyone but Bubba.

"I don't feel like entertaining anyone right now," I mumbled. "I'm sleep."

"Man, get yo ass up and come answer this door!" shouted Shakey.

Damn, he's got the two stooges with him too. They ain't gonna leave until I opened this door.

"Man, do y'all know what time it is?"

"Yeah, we know what time it is—do you?" said Bubba as he barged inside—Shakey and Compulsive following close behind.

Compulsive dived on my sofa and grabbed the remote. Shakey walked over and started drinking the coffee I had just poured in the cup.

"Dog, this shit taste like mud," said Shakey and spit the coffee into my sink.

"That's because I didn't put any sugar in it, Fool."

"Daaaaamn!" shouted Compulsive. "Nigga what happened to your eye?"

"Tee, what happened?" asked Bubba. "Did you get jumped last night? Is that why you didn't show up at work?"

"Nawh man, I didn't get jumped. Me and Rachel got into it."

"Well it looks like you got the worse of it," said Compulsive.

"Yeah, she went ballistic on my ass last night, and it's all your fault," I said to Bubba.

"Why is it my fault?"

"Because she saw me driving your sister around in the car she bought me."

"Did you tell her it was my sister? I can't believe she got this mad over something as simple as you driving someone around in the car."

I didn't tell Bubba that Rachel really got mad because she saw his little sister grab my dick and kiss me. He wouldn't have handled that well.

"Yeah I told her Tangy was your sister. She wasn't tryin' to hear that. She started sayin' I disrespected her and some other crazy shit."

"I told you not to accept that car from her," shouted Shakey. "That's how she keeps control over you."

"For real," said Compulsive, echoing Shakey's sentiment.

"Shut the hell up!" I said to both of them. "If someone bought either one of you a car—especially a Jag—y'all would ride around in it until the wheels fell off."

"I wouldn't," said Shakey. "I'd ride a skateboard to work before I let some chick have control of my transportation. The first time she gets mad at you she's gonna try to take the keys from you."

Shakey had no idea how right he was. Still, I wasn't about to admit that Rachel had already taken the car, and then returned it within a twelve-hour period.

"A woman bought me a Mercedes once," said Compulsive. "I gave it back to her because I didn't like the color."

"Shut your lying ass up, Compulsive," said Bubba. "Damn, Nigga. You wake up lying."

"Whatever, Fool. I ain't lying. Anyway, Tee, did you just let her beat your ass like that?" asked Compulsive.

"What else was I supposed to do? I couldn't hit her back."

"Bullshit!" shouted Shakey. "You should have knocked her ass out!"

"Yeah, Dog. If she came at you like that then she was asking to be treated like a dude," said Compulsive.

"Man, I can't hit a woman," I replied.

"Bullshit!" Shakey shouted again. "My mama told me that if a woman starts acting like a dude, I have the right to treat her like a dude. She used to tell my sisters the same thing. She told my sister's that the moment they raised their hands to hit a man, they needed to be prepared to deal with the consequences."

"I agree with Shakey dog," said Compulsive. "There ain't no way in the world I would have stood still and took an ass whipping like this. Why didn't you leave or somethin'?"

"Nigga if I could have left I would have," I barked.

"I wouldn't have left either…not until I beat her ass," said Shakey.

"So that's why you missed work," said Bubba. "Chauncey was pissed off at you, but I calmed him down. I told him you had an accident. I thought it was a lie, but it looks like that was the truth."

"Yeah he had an accident alright," said Compulsive. "He accidentally forgot to move out of the way of that chick's fist. Nigga, she must hit hard. You look like you caught a right hook from a man. Shakey, she would've knocked your little scrawny ass into a coma."

"Shiiit, y'all crazy. I ain't on that chivalry crap. I wouldn't hit a woman first, but if she raises her hand to hit me, I'ma fuck her up. Period. These bitches think they can just do what they want to a brotha these days and get away with it."

I left the Three Stooges in my living room while I went and took a shower. I didn't want to hear their opinions anymore. All I wanted to do was soak my wounds and figure out how to make things right with Rachel.

Two Weeks Later

31

Kim

This was one of the weirdest days of my life. My professional and personal lives were on a collision course. A slew of discoveries left me wondering which way was up.

The day was hectic from the very start. The Chairman of the Board was at Boxxmore Headquarters to attend a Strategic Planning meeting. I'd missed two straight days battling flu-like symptoms, and my work load had backed up severely. Rachel was clearly annoyed by my absence during such an action packed week so I knew that I had to work extra hard to catch up on projects and restore her already tenuous confidence in me.

There must have been twenty unopened letters waiting on my desk.

During the lunch hour, all of the executives, including Rachel, left to go have lunch at some fancy restaurant. I was glad they were gone. It gave me a chance to catch up and also check my personal email.

Most of the letters were from vendors lobbying to meet with Rachel. The others were from some charitable organization trying to get a donation. The remaining two were for Rachel.

After opening the last few I turned to throw the pile of opened envelopes in the trash when one fell to the floor. I must have overlooked it in my haste to sift through the letters.

"What is this?" I mumbled.

The letter was addressed to Lecar Biko. I'd heard about the letters from bill collectors with Rachel's ex-husband's name on them, but this was the first one I'd seen. Rachel told me I should place all of those letters in a folder and give them to her, but I'd never had an opportunity to do that.

I looked over both of my shoulders to see if anyone was around. I wanted to open that letter so bad I could feel my nipples getting hard. Voices started speaking to me—that good voice and that mischievous one.

You know it's not right to open that letter, Kim, said the good voice.

She ain't gonna know. It's been over four months since you started working here, and she's never asked you about a letter addressed to Lecar, said the mischievous voice.

Don't open that letter Kim, you are playing with your job, said the good voice.

This woman is about to marry your brother and neither of you know anything about her past. Todd could be stepping into a volatile situation that he may not be able to get out of, said the bad voice.

After much thought, I decided to listen to that mischievous voice whispering in my ear. I opened the letter, and all hell broke loose.

December 3, 2002

Dear Lecar,

We have tried to contact you via telephone and mail, to no avail. This is our final attempt to settle this matter with you. Your medical bill balance remains at $19,786. We have not received a payment from you in ten months. We have turned this matter over to our Legal Department and requested that they begin the process of pursuing legal action.

You can avoid litigation by making a payment of no less than 80% of the balance before January 5, 2003. We will accept a payment of $15,828 in the form of a cashiers check on or before the aforementioned date. Upon receipt, a payment plan will be instituted to settle the remaining balance.

This is you final opportunity to resolve this matter. Please contact me at my office upon receipt of this letter. Thank you.

Michele Lowerton
(888) 123-0808 (ext: 234)

My mouth flew open. I was shocked to read that a woman who appeared to have everything was running from such a large debt. And this was the only debt I knew about. I wondered what other outstanding balances were floating around out there.

I could feel a migraine headache starting to kick in as I pondered my next move. Should I tell Todd about this huge medical bill? He needed to know about this. But, how could I tell him about it without Rachel finding out that I snooped and read one of her personal letters. I would surely be fired, the same way Megan had been let go a few months earlier.

I could feel my left temple start to throb. Whenever I got a migraine my eyes would begin to water and the vein that runs along the left side of my head would start to protrude and pulsate. I quickly grabbed a few of the pills my doctor had subscribed.

It would take an hour or so for the pills to start working. In the meantime, I still had to figure out how to handle this bombshell that had just landed in my lap. I was scheduled to start the Management Development Course during the first week of January. I'd worked so hard for this—despite Todd's insistence that he'd pulled some strings on my behalf.

Todd's nose was so wide open when it came to Rachel that there was a strong possibility he wouldn't care about her debts anyway. I would have exposed myself to Rachel's wrath for nothing. I needed to let this discovery marinate for a few days before I said anything.

I left the office late that evening and went to that same Subway restaurant where I'd first run into Todd. I was too tired to cook dinner for one, so I was determined to grab one of those foot-long Tuna sandwiches—that would surely tie me over for the evening.

As I left the store and was walking back towards my car, I heard someone call my name.

"Kim!" shouted the deep voice.

I turned around and saw Big Bubba coming towards me. He looked like a big rhino as he approached.

"Wuz up, Kim?"

"Oh hey, Bubba. Where'd you come from?"

"I was coming outta the pizza joint. Did you got one of those healthy sandwiches?"

"Yeah, I'm trying to watch my weight."

"Shiit, Girl. You ain't gotta worry about getting fat. No disrespect, but you a loooong way from overweight," Bubba replied, and scanned my body from head to toe—stopping a little too long to stare at my butt for my taste.

"Take a picture, it will last longer," I said sarcastically.

"Oh my bad, Baby Girl. I didn't mean to stare, but you got it goin' on."

A part of me wanted to curse him out, but it had been so long since a man gawked at me that I actually smirked at his lewd comment.

"Hey, Kim. I was wonderin' if I could rap to you for a second."

"Bubba I really don't have the time right now."

"Wait, wait, Sweetheart. I know I usually flirt with you and stuff, but I'm not tryin' to come on to you right now. What I want to talk to you about involves Todd."

"What about him?"

"Well, I know I'm violatin', but Todd's my boy and he ain't tryin to hear nothin' about Rachel."

When I heard Bubba mention Rachel's name, he totally had my attention. I went and placed my bag of food and purse on the front seat of my car, and sat on the hood to talk to Bubba.

"What about Todd and Rachel?"

"Well, I don't know if I'm trippin', but every since he started kickin' it with that chick he's been different."

"Yeah I know—he's in love. You know they are talkin' about getting engaged."

"I know! That shit tripped me out. They've only known each other for a few months. I asked him if he'd fallen and bumped his head."

"That's what love will do. It will make even the most rational people do irrational things. Talkin' about engagement after dating a few months is downright crazy. I know that it's happened with other couples and in some cases it works, but I still think it's crazy."

"I agree. I've known Todd for a few years now, and I've never seen him act this way about a woman. But, that's not the main thing that's trippin' me out."

"Well what is it?"

"Since he's been dating her I've noticed he stays injured. Either he's limping because she fucked up his leg. Or he's got bruised ribs or a hurt hand – somethin' is always hurt on him."

"What are you saying?"

"I'm saying that I think there might be some domestic violence jumping off."

My first reaction was to get defensive. My brother and I may have had our problems, but I knew him well enough to say with confidence that he wouldn't beat on a woman.

"Bubba, you're trippin'. My brother would not hit a woman. Not after what he and I witnessed growing up. Todd wouldn't do that."

"Yeah, he told me about what happened to y'all's mom. I don't believe he'd go out like that either. Honestly Kim, I don't believe Todd is the initiator. I know this is gonna sound crazy, but I believe Rachel is beatin' my man up."

"Get outta here," I said dismissively. Bubba sounded like he'd been watching one too many episodes of Cops or one of those other crazy television shows.

"Bubba you can't be serious?"

"I'm dead serious," he replied. "Dude be havin' bandages around his ribs and shit. He's already admitted that he and Rachel have had some physical altercation, but he tries to downplay it.

"About two weeks ago he missed work. I had to talk the club owner out of firing him."

"Why did he miss work?"

"I don't know, but somethin' happened. We had three different parties at the club that night. The place was packed. Todd loves to work on nights like that—that's when he makes the most money in tips. Dude didn't show up for work. He didn't even call. The club was one bartender short. The damn line was wrapped around the club, and the owner was pissed."

"Did you check on him?"

"Me and the fellas went to his crib the next morning. Kim, Tee had a black eye!"

"What?"

"That was my reaction. I was ready to go kick somebody's ass. At first he didn't wanna tell me what happened. I figured he got jumped by some dudes or somethin'. He never did tell me what happened, but I figured it out."

"How?"

"When he went to the bathroom I noticed a dozen yellow roses sitting on his kitchen table. I looked at the card attached - it was from Rachel."

"What did it say?" I asked as I immediately thought back to the day Todd sent Rachel the dozen yellow roses.

"She was apologizing for something," said Bubba. "I don't know what happened, but whatever went down she was the reason behind it."

I was stunned by Bubba's comments. Could Todd actually be being beaten by Rachel? I simply could not wrap my mind around that notion.

"Look Kim, I know you and Tee got some unresolved issues. Some stuff that started years ago. But, I think you need to check on your brother."

"He's not gonna open up to me. Todd and I have never really had that type of relationship," I replied.

"Well he needs someone to talk to. That chick got his nose wide open. I peep her game. She got him blinded by that money. She bought him that car. She's financing his book. She's always breakin' bread with him. Todd keeps a wad of cash in his pocket. She's buying his affection.

"Don't get me wrong, she looks okay, but I've seen Todd pull a lot better lookin' women than Rachel. The only difference is that those chicks that hang out at the club are broke. Half of them have just enough money to get through the front door, and buy one drink. They spend all their time in the club flirtin' with brothas so that they can get free drinks all night. The shit is a sad sight.

"But, Rachel got that paper. Todd ain't never had a woman take care of him like that. Your brother's a kept man. He's not opening up to me. Y'all may be beefin', but I know how he feels about you. He'll talk to you."

I didn't respond. I just gave Bubba a hug and got in my car. I thought about Bubba's remarks all the way home. I was even more confused at that point than I was before I left my job. I had evidence that Rachel was in debt. My brother wasn't financially stable enough to inherit someone else's financial headaches. Now Bubba had just raised another red flag.

My head was starting to hurt even more from the stress. I stopped at a local drug store to get some Tylenol. While standing in line I picked up one of those Seek-and-Find puzzle books. I'd always loved playing those in my spare time. My mother was addicted to them and I felt closer to her when I played them.

After I paid for the pills and puzzle I walked out of the store. Just as I was opening my car door I heard someone else call my name. This time it was a female voice.

"Kim," said the woman. "Kim, right?"

I sighed as I turned around. I really didn't feel like talking to anyone. All I wanted to do was go home; eat my sandwich, pop a few pills, sip on some wine, and play my puzzle until I fell asleep.

"Yes, I'm Kim," I replied. "Megan? Megan is that you?"

The voice calling my name belonged to Megan—the woman I'd replaced at Boxxmore. Her hair looked like she'd just rolled out of bed. Her eyes were blood shot. And she smelled like she hadn't taken a bath in weeks. I wasn't sure if her drug of choice was crack, meth, heroine, or all of the above. But, I was sure of one thing—she was a junkie.

"Yeah, it's me Megan. Remember me from Boxxmore? I saw you in the store. I thought that was you."

"Yeah, I remember you," I replied as I opened the door and stuck my leg inside hoping she'd get the hint that I didn't want to talk.

"How are they treatin' you over there?"

"It's all good."

"How is Rachel treatin' you?"

"Umm, Rachel is fine."

"Hmm. Have you noticed some suspicious things about her life?"

"Excuse me?" I replied.

"Have you peeked at her mail? You should do that some day."Megan looked bad—real bad. I was ready to end that conversation with the quickness. She had been released by Rachel, but she was still asking questions about the woman who'd fired her.

"Checked her mail—have you done it? She doesn't like anyone lookin' at her her personal letters. Especially the one's addressed to her ex-husband. You ever wonder why?"

"Maybe it's because it's no ones business. Anything addressed to her ex-husband is between her and him."

"Has he been around yet?"

"No he hasn't. Why?"

"I just asked. I doubt if he will ever come around there."

"Why do you say that?"

"Because of what she had done to him. I'll bet she ain't tell you all of that."

"What in the hell are you talkin' about, Megan?"

I guess my tone scared her because she took a step backwards.

"I'm just sayin…"

"That's just it; you ain't sayin' much of anything!"

"All I'm gonna say is, she's got secrets. The moment you find them out—and you will—she's gonna get rid of you. Watch her—that's all I'm sayin'. Keep you eyes open, the truth is right in front of you. Watch out for Lecar. He's dangerous."

"Oh, really. How do you know this?"

"I'm confidant about what I know. Rachel knows I found out what she did. Don't think I walked away empty handed. Trust me, I got paid, and I'm still getting paid—from Rachel. She's been paying me to keep quiet since I left.

"But you know what; I'm not sayin' another word. You are obviously her little puppet. I'm gonna let you figure it out on your own."

Megan got into an old Ford Tempo with two other grungy looking drug addicts. They pulled out of the parking lot like they'd just robbed the drug store. I was left standing there with yet another piece of incriminating evidence about Rachel.

I went straight home and started to wind down. Naturally, Todd and Rachel was the centerpiece of my thoughts. Should I get involved in their lives or should I mind my own business? Should I jeopardize my own career growth by snooping into Rachel's personal affairs?

Bubba encouraged me to call Todd. Megan, even though she was high as a kite, encouraged me to investigate Rachel more. Now my conscious is talking to me. As much as I hate to admit it I can see where this is heading. My life is about to change again.

All I could think about as I sat in my bed channel surfing was that letter I'd read and Megan's remarks. I opened my purse and pulled out the letter addressed to Lecar. I read it three more times before I finally decided to call Todd and talk to him about my discovery.

Hello.

"Todd, what are you doing?"

I'm heading to Rachel's house. She rented some movies and I'm going to go over and watch them with her. What's up?

"Turn that radio down please. I need to talk to you about her."

Todd turned down his car radio. *What's up? Are you going to try to talk me out of marrying her?*

"Yes and no. I'm not sure if you should do this—at least not now. Not until you find out more about her past."

I have a lifetime to learn more about Rachel. Besides, how much does anyone really know about their partner's past? People tell you what they want you to know. Rachel and I could be married twenty years and there will be things about her that I don't know. We all have skeletons in our closets Kim – even you.

"Todd, I didn't call you to talk about my past. I called to ask you about Rachel's past. Do you know that she's heavy in debt?"

Kim, what are you talkin' about?

"I'm talking about the bill collectors that are chasing her. She's receiving bills at the job. Today I opened one of them and it said she owed nearly $20,000."

Kim, I can't believe you are around there snooping. You never could mind your own business. Even when we were kids you were nosey. If Rachel finds out you are reading her personal mail she's gonna fire your ass. And I'm tellin' you now, I ain't gonna try to stop her.

"Let's keep it real. If Rachel wanted to fire me you couldn't stop her anyway. She's got your nuts in her purse."

Whatever. You're going to find your ass unemployed—just like that woman that had the position before you.

"Speaking of my predecessor; I ran into her today. She told me that I should check into Rachel's past. Whatever she found out about Rachel that prompted Rachel to fire her must have been serious because she said Rachel has been paying her to keep quiet."

You've been watching too many mystery movies. Rachel ain't payin' hush money to anybody.

"How do you know?"

Because I know.

"Well since you know that, have you learned anything else about her ex-husband, Lecar? My predecessor told me he's dangerous."

I ain't worried about that fool!

"You can try to be brave if you want, but I'm telling you - watch your back. That man has been quiet for a reason. I got a feeling he's about to show up and cause problems."

Are you finished?

"Yes, I'm finished. But I want you to promise me that if you get a chance to find out some more details, you will."

Yeah. Yeah.

"I'm serious, Todd. Promise me you won't ignore the truth."

I promise. Now I gotta go—I'm pulling up in front of her house now.

I had an eerie feeling when I hung up the phone. Todd was as stubborn as a bull—just like his father. Rachel had blinded him to who she really was. I knew he didn't really want to hear what I was saying, but I still needed to speak my mind.

I grabbed my Seek-and-Find puzzle and started tackling the first one. I had to find the names hidden. I scanned all of the names and wouldn't you know it, one of the names on the list was *Rachel.*

I have to deal with Rachel every day, I'm not about to go searching for her name first.

It didn't take long for me to find most of the forty names in the puzzle. When I went back to the beginning to search for the last name left on my list—Rachel—my puzzle had so many circles on it I could barely identify any letters that weren't circled.

Just as I was about to circle it, I figured out what Megan was saying. The revelation left me paralyzed. I thought back to the letter, Megan's comments, Bubba's remarks, and something Danielle said.

I started to retrace every odd comment or experience I'd had while working at Boxxmore. Who was the one person at Boxxmore that knew the most about Rachel and Lecar? Who was the one person that Rachel disliked the most? Megan said the truth was right before my eyes—right in that office. I looked up from my puzzle and mumbled, "Oh shit."

32

Todd

I knew Kim had good intentions, but she was starting to get on my nerves. I believed she was a little jealous that she didn't have a boyfriend or someone to occupy her time. Seeing me happy must have been eating away at her.

I rung Rachel's doorbell, anxiously awaiting my queen. When she opened the door, I wasn't disappointed. Rachel was wearing a pair of daisy duke shorts.

She's got to stop teasing me like this. My heart, penis, and balls can't take much more.

"C'mon in," she said.

I gave her a hug and then went inside. "Where is Cupcake?"

"I sent her over to the babysitter's house. She's going to spend the night."

"Oh really?"

"That's right. I didn't want her to be around tonight. Things may get a little loud."

A huge grin crossed my face. I had been let down before by Rachel so I tried to control my enthusiasm. She was the ultimate tease, but something was a little different about her this night.

"Is the movie so scary that it's gonna make you scream?"

"There may be screaming before the night is through, but it won't be because of a movie," Rachel replied with a devilish grin.

Awwh shit, that's what I'm talkin' 'bout. Good thing I put a bottle of my ginseng in the car. I got a feelin' it's gonna go down tonight.

"If you won't be screaming as a result of the movie than what is it?"

"Who said I was gonna be the one screaming?" asked and then turned and rubbed her ass up against my crotch.

I found myself stuttering once again.

"Go ahead and make yourself comfortable. I have to use the bathroom."

Rachel left me alone in her living room. When she walked out of the living room, I opened the front door, ran to my car and retrieved my trusty ginseng bottle. I downed that drink in five seconds.

When I went back inside, Rachel still hadn't come out of the bathroom. I noticed a letter opener and a few letters on the counter. At that very moment, Kim's voice started ringing in my ear. She'd encouraged me to snoop if I had a chance. Now was my chance.

I can't deny that I was curious to learn more about Lecar. Based on Rachel's description of him and how ugly their divorce had been, the guy sounded like he might try anything. Kim's comments that he was dangerous didn't make me feel any safer.

One of the opened letters on the counter was shaped like a post card. It was addressed to Rachel. Just as I was about to read the letter inside of the card my cell phone started buzzing.

"Yeah."

Todd, it's me… Kim.

"I know Kim. What do you want? I'm at Rachel's house."

Todd, I need to talk to you.

"You've already said enough, Kim. What's all that noise? "

I'm in my car trying to make it through all this traffic. Todd, I know we've had our issues, but you are still my brother, and I still love you. Please meet me so we can talk.

"Kim, I have to go. Bye!"

I hung up the phone. Kim's ranting was starting to give me a headache. I looked over my shoulder to see if the coast was clear, and then opened the letter.

The letter was from Kim's lawyer. It read…

Rachel,

As you know I'm in Hawaii on my vacation, but I wanted to give you an update on your case. We've solved the last issue. We had your record in California expunged, and we've worked out a settlement with the doctor's office. It's been a lot of work, but I think we've finally covered all of our bases. Lecar is no longer a problem.

The last order of business is dealing with the blackmail issue. Let's meet next week and discuss…

"What are you doing?" asked Rachel. The look in her eyes told me that I'd better come up with a good lie.

"Hey, Boo," I replied nervously. "I was just picking up your mail. It fell on the floor."

"It couldn't have fallen unless you touched it. That letter has been sitting there all day, and it didn't fall. Why are you reading my mail?"

I was busted. It seemed like honesty was the only way to deal with the situation.

"Okay, Baby. You got me. I saw the post card and I actually wondered if it was from your ex-husband. You still refuse to tell me about him so I've been wondering what's up with him. I guess my curiosity got the best of me."

"Oh really?" Rachel replied as she moved closer.

"Yeah baby. I know I was wrong for snooping. Please forgive me."

Rachel walked over to the counter and stacked all of the mail. I walked over to the sofa and sat down. I was embarrassed and ashamed of my actions. She and I had come so far; this would surely set us back.

As I sat on the sofa wondering what I could do to clean up the mess I'd created, Rachel approached me from behind. She grabbed my dreads and yanked my head backwards. I was left looking up at her—with a letter opener pressed against my neck.

"I don't know what you think this is, but you have obviously lost your damn mind. As long as you can breathe, you'd better never let me catch you looking through my stuff," Rachel said. "If I ever catch you reading my mail again I'm gonna cut you from your ass to your appetite."

For a moment I thought I was looking up at the devil. She had fire in her eyes. There was no doubt in my mind that she meant what she said.

"I'm sorry, Baby," I replied in a non-confrontational tone.

Rachel slowly released her grip and turned and walked towards the kitchen.

I rubbed my neck and tried to comprehend what had just happened. At that very moment, something came over me. I caught a flashback to the night my father murdered my mother. I remembered the image of that shiny knife in his hand. It glimmered when the light hit it just like the letter opened Rachel held.

I'm not sure what got into me, but I lost my mind for awhile. I stood up and walked over to Rachel. I grabbed her by the back of her head and then pushed her face-forward up against the wall.

"I don't know what your fuckin' problem is, but that's the last time I'm gonna let you threaten me. If you ever pull a weapon on me again, Woman, I'm gonna make you regret it. Do you understand me?"

Rachel wrestled to get away from my grasp, but she couldn't. My elbow was planted firmly in her back while I had her hair wrapped around my fist. She couldn't move.

"I asked you if you understood."

"Yes," she muttered. "I could tell from the tremble in her voice that she was about to cry."

When I heard her cracking voice my mind started playing tricks on me again. I saw images of my mother crying after receiving a beating from my father. I didn't hit Rachel, but I'd come dangerously close. Guilty feelings started to flood my senses.

"I'm about to go," I said as I released my grip and opened the front door.

"You ain't going anywhere you bastard!" Rachel shouted.

After Rachel's remarks all I could feel was a burning sensation in my shoulder and arm. I turned around and dodged Rachel's attempt to stab me in the head with the letter opener.

I grabbed her arm and pushed her backwards. We knocked a statue off of a wine case located against the wall and then fell on the glass coffee table causing it to shatter. My shirt was saturated in my own blood. Rachel and I wrestled for control of the letter opener.

Somehow we stood up again, and were facing off. The entire scene resembled the night my mother died. Rachel lunged at me again with the letter opener. I grabbed her wrist with my left handed and then swung and punched her in the face with my right fist.

Rachel's knees buckled. I grabbed her by the throat and pushed her backwards. She stumbled and flipped over the same chair she'd knocked me over weeks earlier when she attacked me.

As she was falling to the ground she grabbed me with her free hand. I never released her wrist – I didn't want her to swing again. We were in such close proximity, I was sure my luck would run out.

When Rachel pulled my shirt we both flipped over the chair. I rolled on top of her and we both lay sprawled on the floor. There was even more blood than before. Suddenly darkness surrounded me. I'd lost so much blood that I passed out.

When I awakened, I was in a hospital bed. Kim was sitting next to me whimpering and crying. Her eyes were closed and she was looking down praying.

"God, please don't let my brother die. I know we've had our problems, but he's my brother and I love him. Whatever issues he has with me, I want to resolve them. I forgive him for the things he's said to me too."

"I ain't dead yet, ol' big-head girl," I mumbled.

Kim let out a scream that was so loud it probably awakened the other patients on the floor. She literally dove on top of me and hugged me.

"Kim, I may not be dead now, but you're gonna kill me."

Kim was crying so hard she couldn't reply. Once she regained her composure she slapped me on my arm.

"Ol' stupid boy! You scared me"

"I scared you? You scared me. I didn't know demons prayed."

"Shut up."

"What's going on. How'd I get here?"

"You got stabbed. Rachel tried to kill you. I went over to her house to talk to you, but when I arrived you had already been stabbed."

"Where is she?"

Kim didn't reply right away. She looked away and then cleared her throat.

"Todd, Rachel is dead," Kim replied.

"Dead? What do you mean she's dead?"

"When I arrived at her house, the two of you were lying in a puddle of blood. She had a letter opener lodged in her heart."

"What?" I asked, not believing what I'd just heard.

"The police are waiting in the hallway to speak to you. They want to find out what happened."

"I can't believe I did that. She attacked me. I was defending myself."

"That's what you need to tell the police. Why did she attack you?"

"She caught me reading her mail. She just went berserk. She put that letter opener to my throat and threatened to kill me—all because she caught reading her mail. I don't know why she reacted that way."

"I do," Kim replied.

Kim reached down and grabbed her purse. She pulled out a puzzle book and handed it to me.

"What am I supposed to do with this?"

"That's why I wanted to talk to you so badly. I figured out her secret."

"What secret, Kim?"

Kim pointed at Rachel's name in the Seek-and-Find puzzle. She then pointed out how she'd circled Rachel's name.

"Okay. I see her name. What does that mean?"

"Spell her name backwards."

"L-E-H-C-A-R"

"Remove the letter "H" and Rachel spelled backwards is Lecar. Todd, Rachel is a former transsexual. That's what Megan found out when she read Rachel's mail. She fired Megan and has been paying her every since to keep quiet. That's why no one ever saw Rachel's ex-husband at Boxxmore…he didn't exist."

"But she has a daughter," I said, struggling to look into my sister's eyes.

"Cupcake is adopted. She adopted her when she was a man. That's why they don't look anything alike. I remembered something Cupcake said to me. She said, *my momma is my daddy.* Rachel left the West Coast and moved to Atlanta to start a new life. The medical bills she was running from were the result of all the plastic surgery and the sex change operation she had."

"That's why she never wanted to have sex with me," I mumbled.

"I guess so, Todd. If she'd slept with you, you would have figured out the truth."

"That's why she was so strong," I said. "Awwh man, I don't believe this shit. I kissed her. I mean him. I mean… shit; I don't know what I mean."

"Todd, I'm going to step out and get the investigators so that they can talk to you. But, I need to say something first," said Kim as she stood and paced around the room-her eyes filled with tears.

"What's up?"

"Umm, I – I wanted to apologize."

"Apologize for what?"

"For what happened when we were kids. I did freeze that night. My lack of a reaction that night has haunted me for years. I felt like you blamed me so I became defensive. I just want to say…I'm sorry."

I was surprised by Kim's comment. Her emotions spilled out. Her tears were real. She really did understand my position. What she didn't know was that I understood hers.

"Kim, come here," I said, and offered my hand as an olive branch.

Kim walked over and sat down once again. I reached over and retrieved a few pieces of tissue from the box on the nightstand.

"Wipe your tears. I never liked to see you cry," I said and smiled.

"Thank you."

"I want to apologize to you for the way I acted. I was angry at my father, but I took it out on you. I know you were scared. You didn't do anything wrong. I was wrong for saying those things to you…. dead wrong. I just want us to start over when all this drama passes."

"I agree," Kim replied, and gave me another hug.

I spent the next two hours being interviewed by the police. My sister never left my side. She sat there as sturdy as a rock holding my hand.

After everyone left my room, I had time to reflect on my life. I even had a brief discussion with my mother.

"I guess I kind of broke my promise to Mama. I did hit Rachel, but I was only trying to defend myself," I mumbled as tears rolled down the side of my face.

I could hear my mother's voice reply, *No you didn't. You kept your promise. Now take care of your sister.*

Note from the Author

I hope you enjoyed BEATER. My primary goal with this book was to shine a light on domestic violence. My secondary goal was to bring attention to the rarely spoken of issue of domestic violence against men. I want to make one thing clear—it was not my intent to minimize the amount of domestic violence inflicted on women in this country. I grew up in a household where my father abused my mother for years. I can remember violent scenes from my childhood, as far back as when I was six years old; therefore, I can relate to the plight of women.

Nevertheless, there is no way to ignore the fact that women and men can easily find themselves being abused in a relationship. If you or someone you know is being physically or emotionally abused, seek help from someone—family, friends, law enforcement, and/or counselors. Your life could depend on it.

Brian W. Smith